Why Did She Have To Die?

by Lurlene McDaniel

Published by Willowisp Press®, Inc.
401 E. Wilson Bridge Road, Worthington, Ohio 43085

Printed in the United States of America

10 9 8 7 6 5 4 3

ISBN 0-87406-071-0

For Gil, the spirit of '73, and their Championship Season

One

"ELLY Rowan! Your bedroom is a mess. I need you to pick all of your dirty clothes off the floor and get them to the laundry room. Right now!"

"Aw, Mom." Elly shrugged, avoiding her mother's angry eyes. She scanned the bedroom, trying to see it as her mother did. So there were a few piles of clothes on the floor. And there was a bowl of dried out yogurt on her desk . . . and several heaps of records, magazines, and papers strewn about. It hardly seemed worth getting mad about.

"Can't I do it later? I'm supposed to meet Joy at the corner and walk to school."

"After school, my foot! I need to do the laundry this morning. Do it now."

"But I'll be late!"

"You should have thought of that *before* you let your dirty clothes lie around this long."

Mrs. Rowan turned on her heels and let out an angry sigh as she left the room. Elly knew what she was thinking. Her sister wouldn't have waited until the last minute to get her laundry together. And her room never looked like a disaster area. Kathy was neat as a pin.

Elly had heard the comparison for nearly thirteen years between her and her fourteen-year-old sister. Only fifteen months separated them, but it might have been fifteen years for as much as they were alike. Kathy Rowan. Miss Perfect. Miss Popularity. Miss Everything-You're-Not, Elly.

Elly threw herself across her bed, heaving a sigh and thinking dark thoughts. Even though it made her mad that so much had come to her sister naturally—beauty, brains, and personality—it really wasn't Kathy's fault she was perfect. People couldn't help what life gave them.

Elly surveyed her room. "Maybe it is in pretty bad shape," she mused aloud. A soft knock on her door made her leap off her bed. She began scrambling over the floor, picking up clothes.

"Is the explosion over?" The question came from Kathy. Her pert face peeked into the room. Her cascade of dark hair fell to one side as she tipped her head around the door frame.

Elly nodded, her hands on her hips.

Kathy edged into the room, letting out a low whistle. "Goodness, Elly. It looks like there was a war in here."

"I know all about it!" Elly snapped. She didn't need any one else to say anything about her cleaning habits. Especially Kathy. She gathered up a stack of records and grumbled, "I'm going to be late for first period. Mrs. Wenzel said she'd have my head if I was late one more time."

"Well, let me help here." She grabbed a handful of dirty socks.

"I don't need your help!"

Startled, Kathy hugged a pile of clothes to her chest. "Excuse me for living!"

Immediately, Elly felt sorry she had snapped at Kathy. Kathy couldn't help being favored. It was just the way things were. Elly's hazel eyes tangled with Kathy's sapphire blue ones. "Sorry," she mumbled. "I—I really would like some help."

Kathy sniffed, glared, and then resumed picking up. "Hey, this is my sweater! I thought I'd lost it. It was in your room all this time?"

Guilt grabbed at Elly. Borrowing things without permission was not allowed. It was an unwritten rule between them. Just because they were sisters didn't mean one could use the other's property whenever they felt like it. They were so close in age, height and weight, and only a year apart in school that it would have been easy to use each other's wardrobes, makeup, and belongings. But Elly had never cared for Kathy's preppy clothes and all-American tastes. She did, however, love the fuzzy blue sweater. Since Kathy was asked to babysit twice as much as Elly, she always had more money for clothes and records. "Sorry," she apologized.

"Just don't do it again," Kathy warned. They worked in silence for a few more minutes. "You coming to the decoration committee meeting this afternoon?"

Elly started. "Is it this afternoon?"

"Elly! You're not serious! You know I'm the chairman. Only ninth graders are supposed to serve on the committee. I pulled special strings to get you on it in the first place. Don't tell me you're going to miss the very first meeting?"

Elly felt like snapping, "I never wanted to be on the stupid Spring Dance decorations committee. You didn't do me any favors." Instead she said, "No . . . no. Of course I didn't forget. I'll be there." Then she thought about her promise to meet Joy at the library after school. They had planned to ogle Dan

Richards, Joy's latest romantic interest.

"Well, I should hope not. It's only the biggest event of the school year. And it's only four weeks away. I was thinking about doing a May festival theme. Lots of fresh flowers and daisy chains. What do you think?"

Elly only half heard her. She could have cared less. Naturally, since Kathy was the most popular girl at Lincoln Junior High, everybody on the committee would think it was a terrific idea. Frankly, Elly thought the old cafeteria would look better decked out like a bomb shelter than a garden. But who cared what she thought? Who cared what silly old Elly liked? "Maybe next year," she told herself grimly. She'd be the ninth grader while Kathy would start tenth grade at Leon High. It would be the first time they hadn't gone to the same school in eight years.

Elly thought about how nice it would be to be finally free of Kathy, to finally be out from under her sister's shadow. She would be just Elly and not Kathy Rowan's sister. She couldn't wait!

* * * * *

As Mrs. Wenzel tapped her toe impatiently, Elly frantically searched through her notebooks for her homework assignment. She knew Kathy had been Mrs. Wenzel's star pupil. She knew she'd never been late on assignments. And she'd never lost anything important either.

"I did the homework, Mrs. Wenzel. I—I just can't find it." Her cheeks burned knowing that every eye in class was focused on her, but the notebook refused to cough up the missing report.

"There's only eight weeks of school left, MAYBE you can find it before the term's out." Mrs. Wenzel said with irritation. "Just bring it in tomorrow, Elly." She turned on her heel and paced to the front of the classroom.

Elly slid down into her desk chair, folded her arms, and stared straight ahead. She was so embarrassed. Just another case of being second-best to Kathy!

At lunch time she found Joy primping in the girl's bathroom. "It's about time." Joy scolded.

Elly shoved her books onto a stainless steel shelf. She stepped around two other girls to stand next to Joy in front of the mirror. "Give me a break. It's been a bad day." She dragged her brush through her straight brown hair. The neon lights made her look colorless and drab. She thought of Kathy's chestnut-colored hair. Her hair was so dark and thick and full—like a veil past her shoulders. "Do you have a comb? My hair looks like wet spaghetti."

Joy rummaged in her purse and held out a comb. "Are we going to the library after school?"

"Can't. I've got a dumb decorations committee meeting."

"But you promised."

"I can't help it. Kathy roped me into working on the committee with her. I have to go."

"Who wants to go to the stupid old dance anyway?" Joy mumbled.

Elly gave her a knowing glance. "No one asked you either, huh?"

Joy's irritation turned into a sheepish grin. It was always easier to pretend you didn't want to go than to admit that no one had asked you. "How about you?"

"Get serious." Elly pulled the comb through her hair and looked at herself in the mirror. "I'm afraid my hair needs more than combing."

"Who's Kathy going with?"

"I think she's dropping all the names of the guys who've asked her in a hat and drawing out the lucky one," Elly said a bit sourly.

"That many, huh?"

Elly shrugged. "So who cares? After this

summer we'll be the queen bees at Lincoln."

Joy glanced around the green-tiled bathroom. "Some throne room." They both giggled.

"Come on," Elly said. "The bell's ringing. Walk me to my class. I'll call you tonight with a flash bulletin on the Spring Dance decorations."

Joy rolled her eyes. "I can hardly wait."

* * * * *

"You didn't say much in the meeting, Elly."

Elly shrugged and continued walking next to her sister down the old cracked sidewalk toward home. She rested her books on her hip and breathed in the sweet smell of the late afternoon April air. In a few weeks the entire city of Asheville would be sprouting to life. The surrounding Blue Ridge Mountains would begin to bloom, carpeting the slopes with blankets of spring pastels. "I didn't have anything to contribute."

"Well, you must have had a *few* ideas." Kathy's voice sounded irritated. "Honestly, Elly. I thought you'd have something to suggest."

"The others were doing fine without me." Elly recalled the eager faces at the cafeteria table, turned with rapt attention toward Kathy. Naturally, they had gone for every one of Kathy's ideas. The cafeteria would be transformed into a May garden as Kathy wanted. Kathy had thought she could get several local florists to donate flowers. Elly glanced sideways at her sister. Who would say no to Kathy? Who could stare into those blue eyes and that dimpled smile and tell her no?

"But you're not crazy about the idea."

"Just don't let it look like a wedding—or worse—a funeral."

"It won't," Kathy said. "I'll supervise it personally. It'll be beautiful. You wait and see."

Elly nodded, absolutely positive that it would look perfect. After all, wasn't Kathy in charge?

How could anything go wrong with Kathy's touch on it?

Two

"WHAT are those weird things on your feet, Elly? I've never seen socks like that before!" Mr. Rowan asked his daughter as she set the table for supper.

"Oh, Daddy!" Elly tried not to giggle. She was used to her father teasing her about her wild taste in clothing. "These are the latest thing. Like them?" She pointed her toe and displayed her new socks.

Mr. Rowan finished drying his hands on a paper towel. He rolled up the sleeves on his flannel work shirt. "Hope they came free in a cereal box. I'd hate to think you paid money for them."

Kathy stopped tossing the salad, crossed the kitchen, and kissed her father's cheek. "Hi, Daddy. Did you have a good day at work?"

Elly felt annoyed. Why did Kathy have to butt into their private conversation?

"Fine day, kitten." He used his favorite nickname for his older daughter. "If the spring rains hold off a little longer, we'll get all the foundations poured in the new subdivision by the end of the month."

Mr. Rowan was a construction supervisor for one of the city's largest building contractors. His work depended on the weather. He was a mountain of a man, big-shouldered and broad-chested. His massive arms were used to hard physical labor. Elly thought he was the strongest man in the world. Her favorite photograph was one of her father holding his arms up, in a typical he-man pose. Four-year-old Kathy and three-year-old Elly dangled from each bulging arm.

"How was school?" His question was directed to both of them, but it was Kathy who started a running report first. Again, Elly felt annoyed. She felt very small, almost invisible, every time Kathy was in the room.

"The Spring Dance is going to be fabulous." Kathy gurgled. "We've got all these neat plans to decorate. The cafeteria will look like a garden by the time I'm through with it."

"Who are you going with?" It was Mrs. Rowan who asked as she set a steaming bowl of stew onto the table.

"Why does the school promote dating

anyway?" Mr. Rowan grumbled to no one in particular. "These are only kids. Why rush them into growing up?"

"Oh, Daddy!" Elly rolled her eyes. She knew that her dad felt that she and Kathy were too young to be dating.

Mrs. Rowan patted the back of his rough-skinned hand. "Calm down, dear. It's only a dance, hardly a computer dating service. Wouldn't you rather have them going two by two to the school cafeteria with lots of supervision?"

Mr. Rowan grumbled, but accepted his wife's reasoning, while heaping his plate with ladles of thick, rich stew.

Kathy just looked down at her plate and said nothing. Elly narrowed her eyes at her. She lived with her sister too long not to notice the tightening of her shoulders and the nervous glance around the kitchen. *What's going on, Kathy?* Her parents had noticed nothing, but Elly had. Her senses tingled. Why hadn't Kathy spoken up? She usually did whenever Dad got on his soapbox about dating. After all, guys had been trying to ask her out since she'd been twelve.

"How about you, Elly?" Helen asked. "Are you going with anyone in particular?"

"Didn't I tell you? The King of England is

flying in specially to escort me."

"Mercy. Do I have to plan a meal for him?"

"Naw. We're going out for burgers." Inwardly, she knew that she'd be going with Joy to sit among the other unasked girls of the school.

"Well, I know you two will be the best-looking girls there," Mr. Rowan said. Then his gaze fell on Kathy and softened. "Aren't you going to ask me to buy you something new?" His eyes twinkled.

"Oh could we, Daddy? Could we get new outfits just for the dance?" Kathy came to life with his surprise offer.

"I think I could arrange for Mom to take you out this weekend and do some shopping."

Mrs. Rowan opened her mouth as if to protest, but closed it when Kathy jumped up and threw her arms around her father's neck. "Thanks! Thanks a million. I know just what I want."

"How about you, Elly? Think you can find something to match those socks?"

Elly blushed, twisting her legs under the table. "They have some even weirder than this," she countered, suddenly wanting to dress as outrageously as possible for the dance. "I think they'd be perfect."

"Don't embarrass me," Kathy frowned. Elly

smiled back at her sweetly.

"Never, dear sister. Would I embarrass you? Never." But she felt a little satisfied over Kathy's discomfort. She hoped she really could find something really strange to wear. Not that she liked to look weird. But it would be worth the look on Kathy's face when she saw her at the dance! Worth every bit of the silliness!

* * * * *

Elly paced around her bedroom, unable to concentrate on homework. She couldn't get her mind off Kathy's reaction to their mom's question at supper. "Who are you going with?" Even now, hours later, the memory of Kathy's response kept bothering Elly.

"I think I'd better check this out," she said out loud to herself. She went down the hallway to Kathy's door and knocked. "It's me. Can I come in?"

"Sure."

Elly entered, seeing the pretty pink canopy over the bed where Kathy lay sprawled with papers and books. "What's up?"

Elly surveyed the white and gold furniture and floral wallpaper. The room was a perfect reflection of Kathy—pretty, neat, and smelling faintly of lilac perfume. She settled onto the pink bedspread next to her sister. "Just thought I needed some company."

Kathy eyed her speculatively. "Joy's line busy?"

"That too." Elly picked up a framed photograph of Kathy and herself taken the summer before on their family vacation. They were on the beach. Kathy looked curvaceous and feminine in a two-piece blue bathing suit. Elly looked rather flat and ordinary in her one-piece standing next to Kathy on the sparkling white sand. "Why do you keep this dumb thing around?"

"I like it. Don't you?"

"Not much." Elly set it back on the bedside table. "At supper tonight, when Mom asked about the dance . . . who are you going with, Kathy?"

"I haven't decided yet." Elly stared at her. There it was again! She saw the uncomfortable look on Kathy's face.

"I heard Nick Hepplewhite asked you."

"He's just a kid."

"He's a ninth grader." Elly personally thought Nick was pretty cool. Six weeks before, so had Kathy. So what had changed her mind? "You get a better offer?"

"Maybe."

"Kathy Rowan! You'd better tell me what's going on or I'll start screaming."

Kathy's eyes danced and Elly knew at once she was dying to tell her. Kathy scrambled into a sitting position across from Elly, crossed her shapely legs, and leaned forward. "Promise you won't tell? Cross your heart?" she whispered.

"Promise."

"I mean it, Elly."

"Have I ever told a 'cross-my-heart' secret?"

"Okay. Remember last Saturday when Becky and I went to the movie in the mall?" Elly remembered. "Well, guess who I met there?"

"I give up."

"Russell Canton."

Elly screwed up her face. For a few moments the name didn't register. Then it did. *Russell Canton. The star basketball center for Leon High School!* His picture had been all over the sports section for weeks. He was the star that led Leon to its first all-city championship in five years. "You're kidding?" This was some news. Even for a girl as popular and pretty as Kathy. "So what happened?"

"We sat together in the movie. He bought me popcorn."

"I can't stand it!" Elly flopped backward

onto the bed. "And you never said a word!"

"Well, he's a senior and you know how Daddy feels about dating."

"Yeah. You'll probably be in college before he lets you hold hands." She paused long enough to ponder the idea, then began firing questions at Kathy. "So what's Russell like?"

"Russ," Kathy corrected. "Oh, Elly! He's the best-looking guy I've ever seen. I thought I was going to faint I was so nervous sitting next to him in the movie. I never even SAW the film. He took my phone number afterward in the lobby. He's so tall! I had to tilt my head like this . . . ," she demonstrated, "just to see his face when I stood in front of him. He asked to drive me home. He has his own car. But of course, I had to say no."

"Has he called yet?"

A frown creased Kathy's forehead. "Not yet. But he's been busy with the basketball play-offs. He will. I just know it."

"So are you going to ask him to our dippy little junior high school dance?"

"I might. And it's not going to be so dippy," she defended in a ruffled voice.

Elly wasn't so sure. But the news that Kathy had attracted the attention of a guy like Russ Canton *was* impressive. Again Elly looked at Kathy's excited face. The cheekbones were high, the eyes wide and deep blue, her brows perfectly arched. Kathy's mouth was bow-shaped, the corners in a perky tilt. Dimples showed when she smiled. *Pretty*. Elly thought. Pretty and popular and perfect. No wonder Russ Canton fell for her.

Elly sighed and scooted off the bed. "Well, keep me posted. Tell me when he calls."

Kathy flashed her a dazzling smile. "I couldn't keep it a secret if I tried. I'm glad I told you." The bedside lamp cast a golden glow on Kathy's features.

Elly paused at the door long enough to watch her sister gather her homework papers into neat piles and wondered how two sisters could be so different. Would any boy ever care about her when someone as beautiful as Kathy was always around?

Three

"HE called!" Kathy's quickly whispered words almost made Elly drop her glass of orange juice.

"When?"

"Last night, about ten. Dad was mad about a boy calling me that late, but I did get to talk to Russ for fifteen minutes."

Elly vaguely remembered hearing the phone ring the night before. It had awakened her from a foggy sleep she'd drifted into while trying to concentrate on her English assignment. "So what did he say?"

"He said he might drive by the school someday this week to see me."

Elly stared wide-eyed at Kathy, picturing the sensation it would cause at the junior high school if he did such a thing. "You should have him come to the house."

"And have Daddy give him the third

degree? Russ is seventeen. Dad would never let me date him."

As if on cue, Mr. Rowan swooped into the kitchen. "What's all the whispering about, girls?"

Elly looked down guiltily at her plate of scrambled eggs. "Nothing," Kathy told him.

Their father settled into his chair at the table and reached for the newspaper. It was unusual for them to eat breakfast together since his job often demanded he leave the house before six A.M. "I have to go by the bank for the boss before I go to the site," he explained. "You two need a ride to school?"

"We'd rather walk," Kathy said, a little too quickly.

"Yeah. I'm supposed to meet Joy at the corner," Elly added, wondering how she'd fallen so easily into the scheme with Kathy. She flashed her sister a questioning glance, but Kathy pretended not to notice. They finished their breakfast in silence.

Later, as they walked to the corner, Elly asked, "Did Russ say he might drive by our school today?"

"No. I just wanted to walk."

"In case he did," Elly finished. "You're not thinking of sneaking around with Russ are you?"

"I wouldn't do that," Kathy said. "But I would like to get to know him better. Just for fun. I mean he can have his pick of any girl at Leon High. I don't think he really likes me. I'm just someone new . . . different. You know?"

Surprised by Kathy's honesty, Elly nodded. "I—I guess I see what you mean." They shuffled along and Elly gave her sister a wink, "Still, it is exciting to have a sister who gets the attention of Russ Canton, superstar."

Kathy smiled shyly. "Thanks for standing by me, Elly. Don't worry. I won't do anything dumb."

The two sisters locked gazes and instantly understood each other. At that moment, Elly felt wonderfully close to Kathy. "Heck, what are sisters for?"

* * * * *

"You going out for cheerleading?" Joy asked Elly as she looked over the school bulletin posted in the hallway outside the main office.

"Are you kidding?" Elly wrinkled her nose. "With Kathy head cheerleader this year, I don't want to stumble along in her footsteps. I think I'll join the newspaper staff, instead."

"Aw, come on. Maybe because Kathy's on top of the heap. . . ," she giggled at her own joke, "you'll have an inside track. If you go out, I will too."

"No way. I want to do something that's my own."

"But I can't write!" Joy wailed. "And I want us to do the same activity next year."

"So maybe there's something else you can do besides write. Mrs. Wenzel is the advisor. We can talk to her after school." Joy thrust out her lip in a pout. "I hear Dan Richards is on the staff," Elly offered, dangling the information like a carrot in front of a horse.

Joy perked. "He is?"

"Saw his name on the sign-up sheet on Mrs. Wenzel's desk."

"Well, I guess working on the newspaper might have its rewards."

"I thought you'd think it was better than cheerleading."

Elly wondered why Joy was so taken with Dan. He wasn't her taste at all. After knowing there were guys like Russ Canton around, Dan seemed immature and childish. She wondered what it would be like to have a guy like Russ Canton interested in her. She almost laughed out loud. Who was she kidding? Guys like Russ were only attracted to pretty girls, like Kathy.

"Wonder if Dan's taking anybody to the

dance? Has he asked Kathy?"

Elly bristled. "For crying out loud, I'm not her social secretary. So far I don't know who's asked her, but I do know she's real picky about who she'll go with. I mean, what if somebody really cool comes on the scene?"

Joy narrowed her eyes suspiciously. "Are you keeping something from me, Elly Rowan?"

Elly's cheeks flushed. She felt slightly guilty. She'd promised Kathy that she wouldn't breathe a word about Russ. Now she'd made Joy suspect something was going on.

"Of course not. It's just that I don't know everything that's going on in my sister's life. I certainly don't know who she's going to the dance with."

"Well, you don't have to get all huffy about it. I just wanted to know if I had a chance with Dan or not."

"Sorry. I didn't mean to bite. But this whole dance thing is so stupid. I don't even think I'll go."

"You can't desert me!" Joy cried. "If we can't get guys to ask us, at least let's go together. We could have a worse evening."

Elly wasn't so sure, but she promised Joy she'd think about it. That night, Elly made a list of all the boys in her school she thought were neat and who'd be returning the following year. It was dismally short. Only Kenny Hughes made it. "Face it," she told herself out loud, "even after Kathy goes to high school, I'll still be one step behind her."

Kenny Hughes. Elly mulled the name over as she thought about Kenny's dark hair and blue eyes. He was all right. Maybe she could get him to take her to the dance. Then she'd feel less like Kathy's kid sister and more like her own person. Her heart thudded in anticipation. Why hadn't she thought about Kenny before? She'd really like showing up at the dance with him. Despite what she'd told Joy, she did want to go. And her father *was* buying her a new outfit. It might just work out if she put her mind to it. "Tomorrow, I'll put Plan *A* into gear. Tomorrow, I'll start getting Kenny to notice me." As Elly climbed into bed, she told herself she'd go to the dance with a date and not with a bunch of girls.

* * * * *

Elly spent a whole week giggling at everything Kenny said. She even dropped a bunch of papers at his feet to get his attention. Finally, he sat with her at lunch in the cafeteria on Friday. Elly sipped her milk and gazed across the table at him.

"You—uh—you're on the decorating committee for the dance, aren't you?" Kenny asked.

"Sure am," Elly said. Things were going better than she'd hoped.

"I hear it's going to be pretty neat."

"I'm doing my share." She smiled broadly at him.

Kenny shuffled his feet and glanced nervously around the crowded room. "You—uh–you finished with your lunch?"

"All done."

"I thought maybe we could go outside before the bell rings."

"Sure." Elly picked up her tray. Her hands were shaking, but she moved quickly and hoped Kenny didn't notice. She was so nervous, there was a knot in her stomach.

They walked out into the bright noon sunlight and wandered onto the special common patio area of the school. The air smelled clean and warm. Sunlight cut jagged patterns across the old cement tiles. Elly studied the tiny blades of grass pushing up through the cracks. *Get on with it, Kenny,* her mind pleaded silently.

"I was—uh—you know—thinking about the dance. Are you going?" He turned to face her, momentarily sidetracked from his thoughts.

Elly tipped her head and gazed up at him. She remembered to flutter her eyelashes like she'd seen Kathy do when she talked to a boy. Kenny's ears turned red. She desperately wanted him to say the magic words and put them both out of their misery. "I haven't decided yet," she hedged.

"Well, since it's the last dance of the year and summer's coming . . ."

Elly gritted her teeth and swallowed hard. Her hands felt cold and clammy. She thought of the new outfit she'd bought—a soft flowered shirt and brightly-colored pants. *I'll look great for you, Kenny,* she promised him inwardly.

"I mean it's short notice and everything . . . but I was wondering . . . if you—uh—well, if maybe you could tell me if your sister has a date yet."

Four

ELLY stared at Kenny, letting his words sink in. Briefly, she contemplated murder, but gave up the idea. They were standing in too public a place.

"If you want to know Kathy's plans, ask her!" Elly turned and stalked toward the girls' bathroom. Behind her, she heard Kenny mumble, ". . . didn't have to bite my head off. . . ."

Inside the bathroom, her anger turned to tears. Elly leaned against the cool green tiles. The smell of disinfectant made her sick to her stomach. But it wasn't really the odor that bothered her. It was what had happened with Kenny. *Stupid!* she told her reflection in the mirror. She had been stupid to think that Kenny might be interested in her. It had been Kathy he wanted all along. It was always Kathy.

Joy ambled into the bathroom. "I thought I saw you rushing in here. Hey! What's wrong?"

"Nothing," Elly said, suddenly resenting her friend's nosiness. "Can't a person go to the bathroom without making a public announcement?"

"Excuse me!"

Elly raked a brush through her hair. She didn't want to tell Joy that Kenny had rejected her. Instead she asked, "Do you know that Kenny Hughes had the nerve to ask me if Kathy had a date for the dance yet? Where does he get off anyway? I told him to ask her himself."

"I thought you looked angry. But you shouldn't get so mad about it. I mean Kenny acted like a jerk, but so what? You don't like him, do you?"

Joy's curious expression caused Elly to shrug, "Don't be ridiculous. He's a nerd and I wouldn't look twice at him."

"So, no real harm done." Joy flashed her a smile. "Are we going to the dance together?"

Elly sighed. "You're the best offer I've had." She forced her voice to sound happy. "Come to think of it, you're the ONLY offer I've had."

"Thanks a lot!" Joy poked Elly in the ribs, but they left the bathroom together laughing. *At least I'm laughing on the outside,* Elly thought.

* * * * *

By Monday, Elly had decided Joy would be an okay date for the dance. She felt sort of satisfied that the great Russ Canton hadn't called Kathy again. He hadn't followed through on his promise to drive by the school to see her, either. *Justice does triumph,* she told herself as she and Kathy walked home in the late afternoon sunshine.

"So, did you decide which frog you are going to kiss and turn into a prince for the dance?" Elly asked.

"Very funny. Actually, I don't want to go with anyone who's asked me. All the guys keep pestering me to go with them. I don't care a bit about any one of them!"

"Tough problem."

"I guess that sounds vain to you, doesn't it? I mean, why can't I just say yes to one of them and go to the silly dance?"

Elly tried to see too many date offers as a problem. "Maybe the right guy hasn't asked yet."

Kathy gave a shrug. "I wish I'd never met Russ Canton."

The crunch of car tires pulling up next to the curb interrupted Elly's reply. Both girls turned at the sound. "Want a ride, beautiful?"

a deep male voice asked.

No one had to introduce Russ Canton to Elly. Nor did she wonder for a minute who the grinning, blond, green-eyed boy was talking to. Elly hung back, as Kathy stepped casually to the side of Russ's black Firebird.

"Russ?" Kathy asked, as if she hardly recognized him. Elly rolled her eyes. Her heart was pounding against her rib cage. Although she'd seen his picture in the paper many times, nothing had prepared her for seeing him in person. She admired her sister's cool. Only the faintest rush of pink in Kathy's face revealed her excitement.

"Sorry I couldn't stop by sooner. The basketball team's been in strict training for the play-offs. Then baseball season started. I'm the pitcher."

"No problem," Kathy flipped her deep brown hair off her shoulders. "I figured you'd make it sooner or later."

"Listen, I'm wasting gas. Get in the car and I'll drive you home."

Elly saw Kathy hesitate. "Oh, that's all right. My sister Elly and I only live a few blocks away. We were just saying how nice it was to walk, weren't we, Elly?"

Elly fumbled for an answer, trying to get her tongue untied. "Your sister, huh? I see good looks run in your family."

Elly turned beet red. Pleasure seeped through her with his compliment, but she noticed that his eyes barely flipped over her before resting again on Kathy. "Come on. Get in." Russ snapped the passenger door open.

Kathy looked at Elly questioningly. Elly refused to budge. She grabbed her sister's arm. "Dad will ground you for the rest of your life!" she muttered under her breath.

"Not if you ride with us," Kathy countered.

"He wants you to ride with him. Not me."

Russ gunned his motor impatiently. "What are you two doing? Voting?"

Kathy giggled. "Your offer includes Elly, doesn't it?"

Elly could have strangled her. "Sure!" Russ said. "Two pretty girls are better than one!"

Kathy flashed Elly a pleading look. Elly fought her better judgment and gave her sister a short, jerky nod of acceptance. Feeling like an intruder, Elly gritted her teeth and climbed into the back seat. Kathy settled in the front and smiled sweetly at Russ. "Thanks for the lift."

Russ popped the car into gear and squealed away from the curb. Elly clutched the arm rest. She prayed under her breath that their father wouldn't see them. *We shouldn't be doing this,* she told herself.

The car was neat, Elly had to admit. It smelled of lime-scented after shave. She ran her palm across the smooth upholstery. She felt a certain importance about sitting in Russ Canton's car, driving down the familiar streets of her neighborhood. While she hoped she wouldn't run into her parents, she half hoped Joy would see them . . . or even Kenny Hughes.

"We live down this street," Kathy said as Russ shifted into a higher gear.

"I know where you live, but why go home yet? Let's go for a ride."

"Kathy we—we really shouldn't," Elly blurted. She had suddenly realized that they were some place they shouldn't be. The thought weighed heavily on her conscience. She watched Russ's eyes focus on her in his rearview mirror.

"I'll go around the block and let you off. Then, Kathy and I can go."

Elly's cheeks burned. She really wasn't wanted. Giving her a ride was the only way Russ could have gotten Kathy to go along. At once, she felt sudden dislike for the cocky driver and the pain of her own humiliation.

"Oh, I don't know, Russ. . . ," Kathy started.

Elly stared straight ahead, wishing she could slip between the cracks in the upholstery. Up ahead, right in front of them, Elly saw a little

36

girl on a bicycle wobbling unsteadily. She smiled inwardly, remembering her own first experience on her bike without training wheels. She'd been determined to ride on two wheels, like Kathy. Her father had cheered her on despite her many spills.

The little girl didn't see them in the car and Russ was concentrating on Kathy. For a brief moment, Elly thought the bike would right itself before the car came any closer. But it wobbled with even more uncertainty. She opened her mouth, but no sound came out. Instead, time seemed to freeze. Everything around her seemed as if it was in slow motion.

Someone in the car—was it her?—shouted, "Look out!" At the last minute, Russ saw the little girl too. Elly braced herself for him to hit the brakes. He whipped the steering wheel to avoid the girl, and the car responded as if it had been shot from a sling.

Elly saw a blur of motion as a lamp post loomed next to the passenger side. She heard a crunching, shattering sound, felt the impact of metal against metal, smelled the odor of burned rubber. She heard a scream, and the world flipped around her in a skidding circle. A wrenching twist of pain burned along her side. A numbing sensation shot down her leg. Finally, she fell forward into a pit of welcoming blackness.

Five

ELLY floated in a gray fog. The sensation was not unpleasant. She felt buoyed on an ocean of air, cushioned and safe. She heard sounds—sirens, voices, grinding, and the shearing of metal. She drew back from the annoying sounds into the wonderful, quiet cloud of gray.

As she swirled through the darkness, she felt a pinpoint of light flash deep inside her eye that made her wince. She smelled the sharp bite of alcohol. She felt hands lifting her. Something rubbery slid over her mouth and nose. Elly slipped deeper into the fog.

Elly saw a darkened room, like a stage, lit by a brilliant white spotlight. Inside the circle of light, Kathy danced. Elly watched, fascinated, as her sister, dressed in a gown of billowing white gauze, twirled and spun in slow, graceful spirals. Elly heard no music.

She tried to move closer to Kathy, but every step she took made Kathy spin farther away across the stage. Elly struggled to call out Kathy's name, but her voice wouldn't work. She waved, but Kathy's eyes were closed as she danced to the silent music. Elly reached out, fighting against the unknown force that pushed her away from her dancing sister. *Wait!* her mind cried. *Kathy, please wait!* The spotlight began to shrink and with it, so did Kathy, melting into the darkness.

From far away, Elly heard someone calling her name. Over and over, the voice called to her. Pulled in two directions—one way by her sister's disappearing shape and the other way by the pull of the voice—Elly hesitated. Then slowly, the voice began to draw her toward itself. "Elly! Elly! It's Mom and Dad, honey. Wake up, Elly."

Elly floated out of the fog. The stage disappeared and she opened her eyes to a hospital room. The first thing she saw were her parents' anxious faces. The first thing she felt was pain. Elly moaned, longing to return to the quiet sea of gray.

"Oh, honey. Honey . . . look at us." Mrs. Rowan begged.

"Don't go back to sleep, baby girl," her father whispered.

Baby girl. Her father hadn't called her that since she'd been five years old and in the hospital with pneumonia.

"My—my head hurts." Her whispered words sounded like a croak.

Her mother smoothed Elly's forehead, which was covered in bandages. "I know it does. But you're going to be all right. You've come back to us and you're going to be all right." Elly heard tears in her mother's voice. *Back?* she wondered. *Back from where?*

"What happened?" Elly tried to move, but her arms felt heavy. For the first time, she noticed that her leg was covered in white plaster and suspended from a system of pulleys. Tubes and needles ran into her right arm. An inverted bottle of clear liquid hung next to her bed from a metal stand.

"You were in a bad car accident. Do you remember it?"

Elly reached through fuzzy layers of memory. She recalled green eyes, bronze-colored auto upholstery, the lush cascade of Kathy's hair. She remembered a little girl on a bike, the lamp post spinning toward her side, the sound of metal against metal. Elly squeezed her eyes closed to block out the pictures. "Yes. I remember."

"You have a concussion and badly broken

leg. The doctors operated on your leg and put special pins in it. But it will be okay."

Operated? Elly struggled to ask the questions that were tumbling in her mind. "How long . . . ?"

"You've been unconscious for a week," Mr. Rowan said. His voice cracked.

A week? Elly didn't believe it! "A whole week? But what about school?"

Mr. Rowan caressed her cheek. His big hand caught in the strands of her hair. "It was a way for your mind and body to rest. To recover. The doctors said you'd wake up. Just like Sleeping Beauty."

She tried to smile at her father's silly idea. She was no Sleeping Beauty. Kathy was the beauty. Elly's strange dream came back to her. "How's Kathy?"

Mr. Rowan pulled away from Elly's bedside and Mrs. Rowan came closer. "S—she's fine, honey." Her mother's voice sounded forced. Elly tried to focus on her mother's face.

"Can I see her?"

"She's in a different room."

"And Russ?"

"He was treated and released."

"The girl on the bike?"

"Just scared. The car missed her."

Elly sighed, relieved. "I—I'm sorry we went

for a ride with him. It was wrong to go without your permission."

Helen shushed her and stroked her arm. "We'll talk about it later, after you've had some sleep."

Grateful, Elly sighed. She *was* tired. She thought it was odd that she should be tired after sleeping for a whole week. "I would like to rest some more. Tell Kathy that I'm sorry. Tell her I'll see her later." Elly felt gentle waves of sleep come over her. She closed her eyes, but not before seeing her parents exchange a long look. They looked sad. It bothered her that she had made them unhappy.

* * * * *

The next time Elly woke up, a nurse was taking her blood pressure. The tight band squeezed Elly's upper arm. The nurse stared intently at the gauge. Noticing Elly's eyes on her, the young woman brightened. "Good morning, Elly. How are you feeling today?"

"Everything hurts. Where're my mom and dad?"

"They should be here soon. They've come every day to visit you since your accident."

Elly felt overwhelmed by the love she felt

for her parents. Tears stung her eyes. "Will I really be all right?"

The black-haired nurse patted her shoulder and unwrapped the blood pressure sleeve. "Yes, you will. Now that you're conscious, the doctor said we could remove the I.V.'s and start feeding you real food. How does that sound?"

Suddenly, Elly was very hungry. "I'd like a hamburger and a vanilla milkshake."

The nurse laughed. "For breakfast?"

"Well . . . at least a milkshake."

"I'll put in your order," the nurse promised. She turned toward the door.

"Wait." Elly called. "Do you know my sister, Kathy? Is she on this floor?"

The nurse smiled, but she didn't meet Elly's eyes. "As soon as your parents get here, I'll send them in. They'll be glad you're up to a milkshake."

Elly watched her leave, puzzled by her strange response. Maybe Kathy was hurt worse than she was. Maybe she was still unconscious.

Confused and afraid, Elly twisted toward the window. She was surprised to see the wide windowsill covered with vases of flowers and potted plants. Elly pulled herself up to read the cards and notes that were attached to them.

"The nurse said you were awake." Mrs. Rowan came into the room with a beaming smile.

"Oh, Mom! Are all those for me?"

"Every one of them. And your friends have flooded the switchboard with calls. This place will be glad to send you home. Then maybe things will get back to normal around here."

Home! For the first time, Elly thought about her house, her bedroom, her clothes. She eyed her cast. She doubted that any of her pants would fit over it. "How am I going to manage with this stupid thing?"

"There's a therapist on staff. She'll be in today to teach you how to use crutches."

Elly wrinkled her nose. "How long do I have to wear it?"

"Six weeks. Maybe eight."

"That's forever!" Elly wailed. "I'll have it on until school's out."

The door opened again. Mr. Rowan entered. His flannel work shirt was tucked neatly into his jeans. "What's all this complaining about?"

Surprised to see him, Elly asked, "Daddy! How come you're not at work?"

"What? And not kiss my baby girl good morning? You've been asleep for a whole week, honey. I can work any time."

Touched by her dad's words, Elly blushed.

Her dad wasn't usually so mushy but he was acting pretty mushy toward Elly. She decided she must have really scared them by being unconscious for so long.

Elly glanced from one parent to the other. They looked tense and edgy. Elly noticed that her mother kept twisting a tissue in her hands. Instinctively, she sensed that something was wrong. "I really am going to be all right?" she asked hesitantly.

Mrs. Rowan patted Elly's hand. *"You're* going to be fine."

The emphasis on you're made Elly's heart begin to thud. "Mom. Dad. How's Kathy?" Thoughts of her sister in a wheelchair drifted through her mind.

The Rowans exchanged nervous glances. Mrs. Rowan leaned closer. Mr. Rowan kept his gaze focused on a spot on Elly's pillow. "How's Kathy?" Elly asked again.

"Honey . . . " Her mother's voice sounded raspy. "We wanted to tell you together."

"She's hurt really badly, isn't she?" Elly blurted, fighting down panic.

"Elly, Kathy didn't make it."

"Make it? Make what, Mom?"

"Kathy died in the accident, honey. Kathy died."

Six

TIME froze. Elly felt air come into her lungs. She saw sunlight slant through the blinds. It cast narrow shadows across the pots of pretty flowers. She stared at a crack in the corner of the wall. At last, she turned her attention back to her parents' faces. Tears had pooled in her mother's blue eyes. Her dad's brown eyes looked frightened and hurt. She said, "I don't believe you."

"It's true, Elly. I wish it wasn't. But it's true."

"You're lying!" Elly cried. "I saw her! I saw Kathy dancing."

"You were dreaming."

"No. I saw her." Elly twisted her head on the pillow trying to block out the horrible words her mother had spoken. She remembered Kathy's strange and graceful dancing. "I tried to follow her over the stage." Tears choked in Elly's trembling voice.

"Take it easy, Elly. Your leg. . . " Mr. Rowan reached to stop the bobbing of the pulleys.

"I don't care about my leg!" A low cry, ripped from Elly's insides. Mrs. Rowan held Elly's arms, making soothing sounds, patting her and holding her. "It isn't true. She's my sister. The pretty one. The smart one."

"She was killed on impact," her mother said. The words felt like hammer blows to Elly's doubts, driving them out one by one. "We—we buried her four days ago."

"You put Kathy in a hole in the ground? You had her funeral without me?" Elly gasped. Her eyes widened. "How could you!?"

Mr. Rowan grabbed Elly's shoulders and shook her gently. "You were in a coma. They thought you might die too. How could we lose both of you?"

Tears streamed down Elly's face. "I'm sorry, Daddy. Oh, Daddy. I'm so sorry."

He held Elly while she cried. Her tears soaked the front of his shirt. When her crying quieted, she smelled the clean smell of his clothing and felt his hard, muscled arms around her. She remembered the photograph of her and Kathy swinging on his biceps. In her mind, she ripped the photo in half. All that remained was Elly. Silly, funky Elly. Ordinary, slightly kooky, a-little-bit-sloppy Elly. Kathy's kid sister. The only child of Mike and Helen Rowan.

* * * * *

Elly went through the motions of the hospital routine. She met her doctor and listened while he explained about the pins in her leg and how therapy would help her walk "just fine" again. She ate the food the nurses brought and she met the therapist. She read her cards and get-well messages. Elly did all the things she was told to do. But from one small corner of her mind, she kept hearing: "Kathy's dead. Your sister's gone forever."

When her parents came that evening, they looked tired and strained. "We can take you home next week," Helen told her.

"I want to go home."

"You've got school work waiting for you there. But in a few weeks, you can go back to classes. There're not too many weeks left in the year, but your teachers didn't think this would set you back too far. You're a good student."

"Yes. At school everybody can sign my cast." Elly made small talk because she didn't know what else to say. She didn't care if she ever went to school again.

"Would you like a visit from Joy?"

Elly picked at her blanket. "Yes. I think I would."

"She's dying to see you." *Dying,* she thought bitterly. What a funny choice of words. "I'll tell her to come tomorrow evening," her mother finished.

Elly wanted to look forward to her friend's visit. But deep down, she dreaded it. All day, she fidgeted, wishing she didn't have to see anybody. But at seven o'clock, Joy came. Her bubble of dark curls framed her face and her eyes were wide, twice their normal size. "Hi, Elly."

"Hi, yourself." The two girls stared at one another.

"Gee, that's some contraption on your leg."

"It looks worse than it is."

Joy glanced around the room. "Did you get my flowers?"

"Yeah. Thanks."

"Your mom says you can come home next week."

"Tell me about it Joy."

A frown creased Joy's face. "About what?"

"My sister's funeral." Elly's tone was flat. She hadn't known she would ask Joy the question. Now that she had, she was determined to hear all about it.

Joy stepped backward and stuttered. "Well, I—I d—don't know."

"I know you went. Mom said the whole school went. You better tell me before I punch you." Her threat seemed silly, with her leg suspended from pulleys, her body unable to move from the bed.

But Joy licked her lips nervously and glanced around the room. "I—I guess it would be okay." She slid a chair next to the bed. "It was very sad." Joy's eyes filled with tears. Elly quietly handed her a tissue. "She had a pale blue coffin with satin lining. And tons of flowers. I never saw so many flowers."

Elly felt detached, as if she were discussing a television show or a book, not the funeral of her sister. "Go on."

"She didn't look real, you know. She looked like a wax doll. But she was still very beautiful. They put flowers in her hair."

"Like a garden in May," Elly broke in. "The way she wanted to decorate for the dance. Kathy would have liked all the flowers."

Joy shrugged slowly. "They let us out of classes at school so we could all go to the service. The minister told us that Kathy was in a garden where the flowers always bloomed and never faded. It made us all feel better, knowing that she'd always have a garden to look at."

It made Elly feel better, too. "We all walked past her coffin and put a flower on top," Joy whispered. "There must have been a hundred flowers. Later—at school—the student council voted to put a special plaque in Kathy's memory in the trophy display case. Everybody liked Kathy. She was very popular." Joy's story stopped. The room hung heavy with silence.

Elly put her arm over her eyes. "Thanks for coming by. And for telling me. I didn't know who else to ask."

Joy rose. "I—I wish it hadn't happened. Do you want me to give a message to any of the kids?"

"No. I'll be home soon. I don't feel like talking to anyone else." Elly heard Joy shuffle out. She lay staring into space for a long time, without really thinking about anything. The fragrance of her bouquets filled the room. She wished someone would take the flowers away. The rich, floral scents somehow made her very sad.

* * * * *

Elly worked with her therapist and learned to handle her crutches. She practiced until the muscles in her arms throbbed from supporting her weight. The nurses wrote their names in colorful letters on the cast, as did her family and Joy. When it was time to go home, Elly's mother brought her a pair of jeans. The leg had been slit so that her cast would fit.

"Very stylish," her mother said.

Elly hobbled to the side of the bed. She tugged on a brightly colored blouse with large pink flowers on it. "Can I go to school Monday?"

"That's only two days from now."

"I just don't want to lie around the house. I'm sick of lying around." Elly felt nervous and jittery. She wanted to go home, but she was dreading it too. She pictured her house. What would it be like without Kathy there?

"I'm fixing your favorite—spaghetti—tonight for supper."

"Thanks." Elly was packed and ready to leave. The nurse helped Elly into a wheelchair and rode with them down the elevator. Outside, the sunlight was so bright that Elly shielded her eyes. It seemed impossible that she'd been cooped up inside for over two weeks.

She thought it would be hard to ride in a car

again, but it wasn't. Her mother drove carefully. She pulled up into the driveway and helped Elly out, holding the crutches until she gained her balance. Elly noticed that the wooden porch needed painting and the screen door squeaked when it opened. Inside, the house looked the same. It smelled of tomato sauce and oregano.

"Welcome home!" A banner was hung across the bottom of the stairs. "We're glad you're home, honey."

Elly shrugged off her mother's hand. She hobbled up the stairs to her room. She carefully looked the other way as she passed the closed door of Kathy's room. "I think I'll sleep for a while," she told her mother. "I'm more tired than I thought I'd be."

Alone in her room, Elly dragged a chair to the window and pushed it open. She stared out at the tree that brushed across the screen. The leaves were dark green and mature. April was gone and with it, the bright color of spring green. The air smelled warm and sultry. Soon, the North Carolina summer would push its way into the city. *Summer.* A sisterless summer. Elly crossed her arms on the sill and rested her cheek against her forearm. Although she had promised herself she wouldn't cry anymore, she broke into tired sobs.

Seven

THEY went to church together on Sunday. It was strange with just the three of them going. The altar was covered with lilies. Elly watched the light spill through the stained glass window behind the altar. It covered the flowers with little rainbow lights. The minister smiled at Elly from behind the pulpit. It made her feel self-conscious.

Mr. Rowan fidgeted with his tie and squirmed in his seat. The hymnal looked tiny in his big, calloused hands. After the service, people Elly didn't even know kept offering their sympathy. By the time they got home, Elly had a terrible headache. Exhausted, she limped to her room.

It was afternoon when Elly finally woke up. She lay on her bed for a few disoriented moments. Then she went down the hall, passing the door of Kathy's room in a wide circle. The door seemed to pull her toward it. Try as she might, she could not keep walking by without wanting to go inside. Finally, she gave in. Quietly she opened the door to the white and gold bedroom and went inside.

The stillness in the room was eerie. Elly looked around at the familiar objects. Everything was neat and tidy. The bedspread stretched across the bed like a fluffy pink satin cloud. Eyelet pillows of white lace nestled in a clump at the headboard. Elly ran her hand up the post at the corner of the bed, feeling the smoothness of the wood.

Kathy's dresser was still lined with her makeup and perfume bottles. Elly squirted the scent of lilacs into the air, then backed off, afraid that the fragrance might touch her. She couldn't bear the thought of it clinging to her skin.

Kathy's records, books, and tapes stood in orderly little stacks. Photographs, stuck to the mirror, stared down at Elly. They reminded her of other times, other places—a summer vacation, the Christmas they'd both gotten new bikes, school friends whose names Elly couldn't remember.

"Elly? Are you all right?" Elly whirled around at the sound of her mother's voice. Her heart pounded as if she'd been caught doing something wrong. But her mother's face looked concerned, not angry.

"I'm fine. I—I just thought I needed to look around."

"I understand. I haven't gotten up the strength to go through her things yet."

Elly saw through a crack in the closet door that Kathy's clothes still hung in neat color-coded clusters. "What will you do with all of her stuff?"

Mrs. Rowan shrugged. "I want you to take anything you want for yourself. I think we'll give the clothes away to the church charity fund. The furniture . . . I don't know yet."

Given away. That's what they were going to do with Kathy. Give her away in bits and pieces. Elly swallowed. "I don't want anything."

"It isn't something you have to decide right now. Someday you'll be glad you kept some of her things. I took her baby book."

For a moment, Elly feared that her mother might break down. She pleaded silently, *Don't, mother. Please don't.* Then she asked, "What's Dad want to keep?"

"He won't even come into her room." There was an edge of bitterness in Mrs. Rowan's voice. "Pretending it never happened won't make it go away." Elly realized that her mother wasn't speaking to her, but saying something she didn't understand about her father.

"I—I think I'd like to go downstairs now." The walls of the room were closing in on her. She felt Kathy's presence everywhere she looked.

"I'm glad you came to her room, Elly."

Elly hurried out, stumbling with her crutches and almost falling head first into the door. The last thing she remembered before shutting the door was the scent of lilacs seeping through the air.

* * * * *

Everywhere Elly went in school on Monday, she felt people staring at her. She heard them whispering behind her back. *Poor Elly . . . So sad . . . What do I say to her . . .* She knew they stopped laughing and talking every time she came into a classroom. She lifted her chin and smiled bravely. By lunch time, her face felt as if it would crack from all the false smiling.

Kenny Hughes volunteered to get her lunch tray and carry it to the table for her. At one time, this would have sent her soaring into the clouds. Now it only made her nervous and hostile. "I can manage fine." But balancing the tray and the crutches was impossible for her.

"I don't mind. Any time you need help...."

"I don't need anybody's help," she snapped.

Kenny ducked his head slightly "Here comes Joy. I'll see you later."

Elly watched him scurry off, almost regretting her snippy tone. Joy plopped beside her. "Spare yourself food poisoning and skip lunch."

Elly twirled her fork in the unappetizing glob of shredded beef and noodles. "I'm not hungry. I have a headache and I wish this day would hurry up and end."

"You could call your mom and go home if you wanted."

"I don't want to go home either," she said through clenched teeth. "I just want everybody to stop whispering behind my back."

"Gee, Elly, everybody's just sorry. We don't know what to say to you."

Elly grabbed for her crutches and shoved her chair backward. "I'm getting out of here. I don't want everybody feeling sorry for me."

"We can't help it. We miss Kathy, too." Joy's eyes looked misty and Elly hobbled away from her before she, too, began crying.

In English class, Mrs. Wenzel welcomed

Elly back and asked if she thought she could catch up. Elly replied that she could do her work and that she'd done extra reading in the hospital. She tried to pay attention during class, but her mind kept wandering. She doodled on her notebook instead of taking notes. By the time the bell rang, Elly thought she'd jump out of her skin. She started toward the door, but Mrs. Wenzel stopped her. "Elly, could you come up here, please?"

She hobbled obediently to the front of the room. She forced a big smile on her face.

"How are you doing, Elly?" Mrs. Wenzel asked.

"Just fine. I think I'll be ready for your test on Friday."

"I mean, how are you and your family doing? I spoke to your mother. She tells me it's been very hard on all of you."

"I tell you, I'm okay." Elly fought down a rising wave of panic. She didn't want her private feelings spilled all over Mrs. Wenzel's desk.

"There are support groups, Elly. . . ."

"What?" Elly shuffled her feet. She felt sweat pour down her arms and pool on the grips under her hands.

"Support groups. People who have gone through the same thing your family is going through. Counselors and kids just like yourself. People who've lost someone close to them."

Elly felt her cheeks flush hot. She didn't want to be talking about this with Mrs. Wenzel. She didn't need any support groups and she didn't want to sit around talking to a bunch of other kids about her dead sister. "I—I think we're doing just fine, Mrs. Wenzel. I think it's nice of you to be concerned for me. But I don't need anybody else knowing right now. I think the whole world knows already." She forced another smile.

Mrs. Wenzel gave her such a probing look that Elly was afraid she might crack. She tapped her crutch impatiently. "I really should be going. It takes me longer to get down the hall with these crutches."

"Of course. But Elly, I mean it. If there's anything I can do to help. . . ."

Elly slipped behind her pasted smile. "Thank you, Mrs. Wenzel," she said. But she thought, *No one can help.*

Eight

ALONE in her bedroom before supper, Elly stared long and hard at her reflection in the mirror. She saw dark circles under her eyes. Despite her blusher and freshly applied lip gloss, she looked pale and thin. "So, is that the best you can give me?" She asked the mirror with an accusing tone. "Where's your smile? Where're your dimples?"

The mirror's sullen reflection glowered at her. *Ugly.* she thought. *Why does my hair always hang so limp and ugly?* Elly tipped her head and picked up a hank of her hair. It hung in a clump from her fingertips. Memories from the past began flooding her.

"Aw, come on, Elly. Just let me cut some bangs."

Five-year-old Elly thrust out her lower lip at Kathy. She didn't want her hair cut. "You'll make it ugly."

"I will not. I'm six years old and I know all about cutting hair. Tell you what, if you let me cut bangs, I'll let you play with my doll."

Elly perked. "The doll with the wedding dress?"

"And the boy doll too. You can have a wedding for them."

Elly looked at her hazel eyes and round cheeks in the mirror. She tried to picture herself with straight bangs. She thought of the beautiful doll that was Kathy's special favorite. How she'd begged to play with it before! Now Kathy was almost letting her. "Well, if you promise not to poke me with the scissors."

Kathy gave her a smile. "I'll be real careful."

Elly watched as her sister lifted the scissors along with a hank of Elly's hair. Kathy's blue eyes danced with delight. The scissors snipped away. Finally, only one tuft of hair was left. It stood straight out from Elly's forehead. Kathy's eyes grew wide and she tried to smooth it flat. The stubborn strands refused to obey.

Elly squirmed. "Can I play with your dolls now?"

"I—I guess so." Kathy quickly slid the scissors into her dressing table drawer. "Uh—Elly. Do you like your bangs?" Kathy nodded as if to encourage Elly's approval.

Elly tipped her head from side to side and

watched the prickles of hair bob. "It's all right. Let's go show Mom."

"No, let's not. You can show Mom and Dad tonight. Let it be a surprise."

Elly shrugged and wiggled off the chair. "Let me have the dolls, Kathy," she pleaded.

"Are you going to tell them I cut your hair?"

"But you did cut it." Elly didn't understand why Kathy seemed nervous. All Elly wanted was the dolls.

Kathy put her arm around Elly's shoulders. "Tell you what. If you don't tell them I cut it, I'll let you play with my dollhouse too."

Elly clapped and giggled. "You will? Oh, Kathy, you're the bestest sister ever."

Elly shook off the mood of the memory. She recalled that they'd both been spanked and that it had taken her bangs two months to grow back. But she never forgot that wonderful afternoon she'd spent playing with her sister's dolls. Now, as her reflection stared back at her, it seemed that her hair was particularly unattractive. "Wonder what it would look like real short?" She asked herself out loud.

A sort of excitement rippled through her as she imagined her hair in short hunks. With a little work, she could make it look very different. She could even dye it afterwards.

Different. Yes, with a little cutting and coloring, she could look very different.

Elly fumbled in her drawer for the scissors. She stretched a hank of her hair outward and thrust the scissors through the light brown tresses. The cluster fluttered to the floor.

* * * * *

"My goodness! What have you done to yourself?" Mr. Rowan stared in disbelief at his daughter.

Elly felt tears sting her eyes. She knew her hair looked awful. No matter how hard she worked or how much she'd cut, she couldn't get it to come out right. She raised her chin and looked straight at her father. "It's not that bad."

"Bad? You look like a circus freak!"

"Mike!" Mrs. Rowan broke in, stepped to Elly's side and squeezed her shoulders. "Let up. I'll take her to my hairdresser tomorrow afternoon."

"Let up?" He exploded. "Why would she go out of her way to make herself ugly. Why?"

Elly trembled, not from her father's anger as much as from her own sense of failure and disappointment. "It's the latest thing."

"Be quiet," Mr. Rowan demanded. "You'd

better shape up, young lady. Hasn't this house been through enough grief without you acting like some weirdo? Cutting your hair like that. What's the matter with you, Elly?"

Her lips trembled, but she refused to break down in front of him. All at once, she hated her father. She hated the way he'd treated her. "I'm sorry you think I'm ugly. I know I've never been pretty and smart."

"Well, cutting your hair that way certainly wasn't a very smart thing to do. Now, fix it or shave it all off and be done with it!" Mr. Rowan gave a disgusted snort and stomped from the room. Mrs. Rowan turned to Elly and touched her arm. "He didn't mean it, Elly. He's just upset and angry. We can fix your hair. But you'll have to wear a short style. It'll be cute on you, honey. Wait and see."

Elly nodded, feeling broken and scattered. Yes, they could fix her hair. But how could they fix what was happening to their family?

* * * * *

Elly woke up from a deep sleep startled. She was unsure what had awakened her. Through the darkened house, the sound of whimpering came to her, making her skin prickle. She scooted out of bed and opened

65

her bedroom door cautiously. At the end of the long hallway, she saw a bright line of light from beneath the bathroom door.

Elly inched down the dark hall. Her heart thudded with uneasy dread. She stopped in front of the door, cracked ever so slightly. The sound of muffled crying made her heart pound faster and her mouth to go dry.

She shoved the door slightly and it inched open. In the glaring white light of the bathroom, reflected in the mirror, she saw her father. He stood against the white-tile wall, his hands covering his face. His body was shaking with racking sobs.

For a few moments, Elly couldn't believe what she was seeing. Fathers don't cry. They were big and strong and brave. And her father was the strongest of all. Elly remembered the time he'd been hurt in a construction accident. He'd been in terrible pain, but he hadn't even complained, let alone cried.

She wanted to say, *Don't cry, Daddy! I'm so sorry I cut my hair. Please don't cry.* But instead, she pressed her back against the wall and hid in the shadows. She didn't want her father to see her or to know that she'd seen him. She knew it would embarrass both of them.

Elly padded swiftly back down the hall to

the safety of her room. Her teeth chattering, she burrowed under the covers. She hugged her pillow to her chest, trying to push aside the memory of her father's tears. "It's my fault," Elly told herself. "It's all my fault." If only she hadn't cut her hair. He had so much on his mind. Now she'd made it worse for him.

She stared straight up at the bare ceiling. "I'm so sorry, Daddy," she said into the darkness. "I'm so sorry."

Nine

"I thought they'd canceled it," Elly said to Joy as they stood staring at the newly painted poster on the school's bulletin board. *SPRING FANCY* was printed in a bright daisy chain of elaborate flowers.

"They just moved it to another weekend. It's the biggest event of the year and everybody still wants to go. So, the administration decided to postpone it." Joy poked Elly's arm playfully. "Aren't you still going to be my date? You helped plan the dance. I figured you'd still want to go. Even if it is with me."

Kathy had helped plan the dance, too. Elly thought of it as Kathy's dance, Kathy's theme, Kathy's committee. No, she didn't want to go. It had only been a month since the accident, but in some ways it seemed as if a million years had passed. She'd forgotten all about the dance until she'd seen the poster.

"Florists are donating bunches of flowers," Joy continued. "The old cafeteria will look like a garden just like . . . " Her voice faded.

". . . just like Kathy wanted," Elly finished. "You don't have to be so jittery, Joy. I *can* talk about her, you know. She's gone, but I'm not going to fall apart at the mention of her name. I forgot about the dance, that's all. I didn't really think they'd cancel it just because . . . " Elly turned smartly on the rubber tips of her crutches. "Come on. We'll be late for class."

The girls walked down the hall, past rows of lockers, through groups of kids milling around. A traffic jam near the water fountain made Elly mad. In a strange act of revenge, Elly planted the tip of her crutch on the sneaker-clad toe of one of the boys. He yelped with pain. "Hey! Watch out or I'll . . . " He stopped when he saw it was Elly. "Oh, sorry. I didn't know it was you." He stepped aside, allowing her to pass.

Elly gave him a smile as if she was sorry for what she'd done. But deep down she didn't mean it. She was glad she'd hurt him. She told herself that if anyone else got in her way, then she'd hurt them, too. Why not? Life was full of pain.

* * * * *

Elly propped her back against the rough bark of the tree. She squirmed for a few minutes, trying to get comfortable so that she could study. The cast bothered her more and more lately. She shoved the end of her pencil inside the opening at the top. She couldn't reach the itch she was trying for.

"What if it falls down inside?" The question came from Kenny Hughes and startled her. Elly glanced up at the dark-haired boy. Afternoon sunlight framed him against the blue sky and sent sparkles off his dark brown hair.

"Aren't you supposed to be in phys ed?"

"I'm taking a break. The coach doesn't care. Besides I'm better with the soccer ball than anybody else out there." To prove his claim, Kenny dropped the soccer ball he held. He bounced it several times off his toes and knees. It didn't hit the ground once.

"I'm impressed," Elly said with a bored tone. She ignored him and opened her English book. He still didn't leave. Instead he plopped down under the tree next to her.

"You—uh—you studying?"

"Aren't you clever? Picked right up on it, didn't you?"

"You know, Elly, you've got a real mean mouth on you lately." Kenny's blue eyes narrowed.

The truth in his words embarrassed her. She gave him a half-hearted shrug. "I don't know why I sounded so nasty. I didn't mean to." She smiled weakly at his glowering stare. "Sorry."

He leaned back on his elbow and spun the soccer ball on the tip of his forefinger. "So when's the cast come off?"

"A few more weeks. Then I have to build up my leg muscles again. The doctor says it'll take awhile."

"Playing soccer would help. I could show you some moves."

She grinned shyly. "I don't think I can start with soccer. The doctor says I need to be careful at first. I don't want to break it again."

An awkward silence filled the space between them. Kenny cleared his throat. "I kind of like your hair short that way."

Elly touched her super short haircut knowing that it was the best her mom's hairdresser could do with the butcher job she'd made of it. "Thanks. I was getting tired of long hair."

"Look, Elly," Kenny licked his lips and stopped spinning the ball. "I've been wanting

71

to tell you something for a long time. I acted like a real jerk that day in the cafeteria . . . about the dance and all."

Elly's mouth went dry. She'd tried to erase forever the day they'd discussed the dance, when she'd wanted him to ask her more than anything in the world. Then he'd asked her instead to help him get a date with Kathy. She wondered if he knew that the tops of his ears turned red when he was embarrassed. "It's not important," she said. "All the guys wanted to ask Kathy."

"It's important to me that you know something." Kenny rubbed the palms of his hands over his dangling shirt tail.

"I wouldn't have asked Kathy to the dance. I don't know why I said such a stupid thing to you."

Elly traced a pattern in a deserted ant hill, making lazy loops with a small stick. "It's okay. I mean, you couldn't help wanting to take her."

"But that's just it. I didn't really want to ask her." She snapped her head up at his comment. Elly looked up at him with a doubting look on her face. Kenny added hastily, "Look, I'm still not saying what I want to say. I'm sorry for the way I acted and I was wondering . . . you know . . . if you weren't going with anybody else—well—maybe you'd go with me to the dance this weekend."

He'd said the last part so fast, Elly almost didn't catch his words. She stared up at him. "I can't dance, Kenny. I have a broken leg," she said, feeling incredibly stupid about pointing out the obvious.

"So what? I don't have a broken leg and I can't dance either."

Elly giggled. If she accepted, their relationship would change somehow. Two months before, she'd wanted that more than anything. Now, it frightened her. She remembered the outfit she'd bought for the dance. She'd have to slit the slacks so her cast would fit. And then there was Joy. . . .

"Well, what do you say?"

He reminded her of an anxious puppy. Something melted inside her and she nodded. "All right. Sure. That'll be fine."

Kenny's face broke into a wide grin. "Cool. We'll have a good time. My mom will have to drive us because of your cast, but we'll have a real good time."

For the first time in weeks, Elly smiled an open, honest-to-goodness real smile. He helped her to her feet and handed her the crutches. Together they walked back toward the gym.

* * * * *

"Yeah. That's real neat." Joy said after
school when Elly told her about her date to
the dance. But she didn't sound very
enthusiastic to Elly.

"I thought you'd be happier about it."

Joy kicked a clump of dirt across the
sidewalk. "But now I don't have anyone to go
with. I'll be standing around all night with no
one to talk to."

"Well, it's not like I'll be dancing all night,
you know. I'll be doing an awful lot of standing
around, too."

"Sure. But you'll have someone special to
stand around with, and I won't."

They walked on in silence. Elly realized that
another gulf had opened between her and her
best friend—first Kathy, now the date. Elly
felt suddenly lonely and isolated. She'd have
no one to help her get ready. Kathy would
have been excited for her. She would have
giggled with her, helped her fix her makeup.
But Kathy was gone. There was no one else.

* * * * *

Mr. Rowan frowned at Elly's news about the
dance at the dinner table. "It doesn't seem

right," he said. "You going out dancing...."

"I won't be dancing!" Elly practically shouted.

"Mike. Elly," Mrs. Rowan interrupted. "Stop it. Elly had planned to go to the dance ages ago. You bought her a new outfit, remember? Why shouldn't she go?"

"It just doesn't seem right," Mr. Rowan muttered.

Tears scratched to get out from behind Elly's eyes. "Nothing seems right any more. I never do anything right for you." Her hands were shaking.

"Stop feeling sorry for yourself," Mr. Rowan said angrily. He scraped his chair away from the table and stalked to the back door. "I'm going out for a drive." The door slammed behind him, and Elly sat in confused silence. It seemed to her that her father didn't care about her anymore.

"Honey," Mrs. Rowan reached for Elly and Elly jerked her shoulder away from her.

"I'm going to my room." She snatched her crutches and limped off. That night, Elly dreamed that she was walking down the school corridors, opening doors, looking for something. In every room, kids sat, facing forward. They turned unsmiling faces her way as she scanned the room for—for what? Embarrassed,

Elly retreated from every room, shutting one door and opening the next, only to be greeted by hollow staring eyes.

She felt panic as she searched and searched the endless hallway of doors and rooms. Her heart pounded, and her palms began to sweat. It grew difficult to move, as if she were pushing against a powerful force.

She awoke, gasping in terror. The cocoon of darkness settled around her. *What was I looking for?* She had no answers. But her cheeks and pillow were soaking wet.

Ten

"THE least you can do is come to the mall with me and help me pick out something neat to stand around in at the dance." Joy's tone of voice made it sound as if it were all Elly's fault that Joy didn't have a thing to wear to the dance that Saturday. To avoid an argument, Elly had gone to the mall, hobbling along on her crutches. All the while, she wanted to be back home.

"What do you think of this?" Joy paraded in front of Elly in the dressing room, wearing a bright outfit—an aqua top and boldly-flowered pants.

She thought it looked better on the mannequin. "I think it looks interesting," Elly hedged.

Joy frowned at her reflection and tugged at the too-tight pants. "I look like a stuffed potato and you know it."

"Okay, so maybe you'd look better in solid-colored pants."

"Thanks a lot."

Elly rolled her eyes. "How about a root beer? All this shopping is making me thirsty."

Joy grumbled as she changed. Then the two of them strolled through the giant mall toward the nearest snack bar.

"Here, go buy me a root beer. I'll wait on this bench," Elly directed, thrusting a dollar bill into Joy's hand. She settled onto the wooden bench beneath a hanging planter of flowers, propping her crutches next to her. Sunlight flooded down from the skylight above, causing the petals of the flowers to shimmer. Suddenly, Elly heard boys' voices behind her. One male voice stood out from all the others. It made her stomach feel peculiar. Her hair prickled along her arms.

"I tell ya, we'll kill West High this afternoon. I plan to pitch a strike-out."

"I don't know, big man," another voice chimed in. "West High's got the best batters in the league."

Elly froze. *Russ Canton.* Her eyes looked in the direction of the voices. Sure enough, there were Russ and his three buddies, less than twenty feet away, tossing down soft pretzels. He was dressed in his baseball jersey and it stretched tightly across his muscular shoulders. His blond hair trailed over his forehead. His hands were large and powerful—an athlete's hands. She remembered them on the wheel of his car.

"Listen, those guys won't know what hit them. Coach clocked my fast ball at 75 miles an hour." *"I know where you live. Let's go for a ride."* Elly trembled and sunk down into the bench, trying to make herself disappear.

"Well, your pitching better be good, Canton. Your batting stinks."

"Look, it's been a rough few months. I'm lucky I made it through basketball play-offs." *"I'll go around the block and let you off. Then, Kathy and I can go."* Elly desperately searched for Joy. Where was she? Why didn't she hurry? The scent of the flowers faded. Elly recalled the tingling bite of Russ's after shave and the cool, smooth upholstery beneath the palm of her hand.

"Come on. We'd better get a move on or we'll be late to the field."

Elly spun, hiding her face. Her cast bumped her crutches, and they clattered to the brick floor. She reached for them, forced down the panic in her throat. As she righted herself, her hazel eyes met Russ's green ones. The image of Kathy Rowan flared between them. They both went pale.

"Hey, Russ, what's the matter? You look like you've seen a ghost," his friend said.

Elly suddenly felt bold. She fixed her gaze on Russ, daring him to look away. *"He walked off without a scratch,"* her dad had told her. *"It was an accident. An accident."* Russ's eyes said to her across the distance of twenty feet.

Elly watched Russ shove his hands into his pockets and turn away. He began to jog away from the bench and his friends. "Wait up, man! What's the matter with you Canton?" Elly followed Russ with her glaring eyes until he disappeared into the crowd. Suddenly, she felt very sick to her stomach.

"Sorry it took so long, but the line was a mile long." Joy offered Elly the root beer. Elly just stared at it stupidly. The ice had melted and a film of brownish water pooled at the top of the cup.

"I hate warm root beer," she hissed, knocking the cup from Joy's outstretched hand. The liquid splashed all over the brick and up the side of the planter. "Can't you do anything right? Don't you know that I hate warm root beer?" Elly thrust her crutches under her arms and limped away. Joy just stared open-mouthed at her retreating figure.

A 75 mile an hour fast ball. A 40 mile an

hour car. Statistics. Two lived and one died. Statistics. One was hurt and one was unscratched. Statistics. Elly held back the tears until she reached the nearest restroom.

* * * * *

"You look cute, honey. Doesn't Elly look cute, Mike?" Mrs. Rowan asked as Elly stood in the living room, ready for the dance.

Elly's father lowered the newspaper and took a swift glance at Elly. "Fine. Just fine."

Elly felt disappointed. He'd hardly seen her. Now if it had been Kathy. . . . A knock on the door meant Kenny had arrived. Elly hurried out, grateful that he'd come to take her away. She decided that Kenny looked terrific in cream-colored corduroy pants and a navy blue sweater. He told her she looked good too, in spite of the cast and crutches.

At the cafeteria entrance, Elly felt a momentary wave of uncertainty. Kenny gripped her elbow helping her through the door and into the dance. Plants and flowers lined the green walls. Baskets of flowers sat in the center of each table. Daisy chains hung from the ceiling and met in the center of the cafeteria. Overhead a mirrored ball spun and reflected colored light onto the dancers below.

A disc jockey, half hidden by a wall of greenery, spun records from the old stage.

Kenny made the rounds, saying hello to his friends. Elly tagged along, wishing she was happier about being here. She saw Joy and waved. Joy smiled and Elly was relieved that she'd forgiven her for the root beer episode. Joy had understood her reaction to seeing Russ Canton again. Joy was a good friend.

"Do you—uh—you think you could dance a little bit?" Kenny's question caused Elly to snap out of her sad mood.

"I thought you said you couldn't dance."

"Well, nothing fancy. But I can fake it through this slow song."

Elly's heart pounded as Kenny took her crutches and slanted them against the wall. He held her hand, slipped his arms around her waist, and touched his forehead to hers. Elly put her arms over his shoulders and closed her eyes. The two of them swayed slightly to the slow beat of the music. The cast weighed Elly down, but also kept her leg from shaking. She'd never been in a boy's arms before. Kenny's grip tightened, and the pressure of his forehead made her lightheaded. His warm breath on her face smelled like cinnamon.

"See, you can dance," he said.

"But I can't play soccer."

"Plenty of time to learn."

Elly felt like she was in a dream. The music ended all too quickly. Shy and flustered, she pulled out of Kenny's embrace. Why did her legs feel rubbery? And why was her heart thudding so hard? Could he hear it? "I think I'll go to the ladies room," she said.

"Sure." His voice sounded husky. "I'll get us some punch and wait for you over at that table." He gestured vaguely and handed her the crutches. She headed toward the restroom. Elly paused at the door, to catch her breath. She heard the voices of two teacher chaperones drift from down the hallway.

"Doesn't it just break your heart?" one said with a thick Southern accent. "Every time I see that sweet little Elly, I almost cry."

"I know what you mean. She puts up such a brave front, but it must be hard on her, losing her sister so tragically."

"Wasn't Kathy a beauty? She had so much potential. It's just awful that she died when she had so much going for her."

They were talking about her and Kathy! They were feeling sorry for her, pitying her! Elly almost gagged.

"Isn't it nice of Kenny Hughes to bring her to the dance?" the thick accent said.

"Oh yes. It would have been doubly hard on

her if she had had to come alone. And this whole evening is such a wonderful tribute to Kathy."

Elly pressed herself flat against the wall and inched backward, toward the room full of kids. She saw the cafeteria in a new light. The flowers, the music—it was all for Kathy's benefit. And Kathy didn't even know about it. All her dreams were to have been fulfilled this night—the perfect dance, a special date with Russ Canton, the adoration of her friends and family, and she would never know. Elly swallowed hard against the gagging lump in her throat.

"Are you all right?" Kenny had come up beside her. A spray of colored lights from the mirrored ball overhead sprinkled on his hair and shoulders.

"Why did you ask me to this dance, Kenny?"

"What do you mean?"

"I still think you really wanted to bring Kathy. You feel sorry for me, don't you? 'Poor Elly,'" her voice mimicked the ones she'd overheard. "'Poor little Elly.' Well, I don't need your favors, Kenny Hughes. Do you hear me? I don't need anybody's favors. I'm calling my mother to come and get me."

Kenny stared at her, open-mouthed. Then

his lips formed into an angry line. "Suit yourself, Elly. Go call your mother! If you really think I asked you because I felt sorry for you then that's your problem."

"Why did you ask me?" Her voice trembled and she held her chin up stubbornly.

"You figure it out, Elly. And when you do, call me. Because I won't bother you again."

She watched him stalk off toward the cafeteria door. Her fingers balled around the hand grips of her crutches until they ached, but she didn't call him back.

Eleven

JOY cornered Elly in the girls' bathroom on Monday just after first period. "So what happened at the dance? First, I see you and Kenny all huggy-poo on the dance floor, then the next thing I see is Kenny all alone and you are no where in sight."

Elly gave her a bored look in the mirror. "My leg was bothering me, so I called my mom to come and get me."

"But your leg's almost healed. Isn't the cast coming off next week?"

Elly ground her teeth over Joy's questions. Joy knew her too well. "Stop with the third degree, Joy. I don't want to talk about it. Did you have a good time at the dance?"

Joy shrugged and answered, "If dropping my cup into the punch bowl and staining my new blouse counts as a good time, then I had a ball."

Elly smiled in spite of herself. She dug in her canvas purse for her eye shadow pencil. She used it herself and then offered it to her friend. "Here. Your makeup looks a little streaked."

Joy smoothed the green pencil over her eyelids. "Thanks. I hate having phys ed in the morning. It takes me all day to recover. Maybe next year I'll get a decent schedule."

Next year. They'd be ninth graders: the queen bees, the top of the heap. The clang of the bell caused Joy to snatch up her books. "I've got to run. If I'm late to math one more time. . . ." She paused at the door. "Are you coming?"

"In a minute," Elly said, combing the short sides of her hair. "The crutches give me an excuse to be late and so I take advantage of it."

"See ya later." Joy fled the bathroom and Elly glanced around, realizing that she was all alone. The quiet made her feel uneasy. She let out her breath in one deep heave. It echoed hollowly off the walls. *Alone.* Elly was all alone. She pushed the thought of Kenny Hughes aside, determined not to think about him or to remember the feel of his arms around her waist.

She stared into the mirror. Her nose had a

bump in its bridge. Her eyes were too far apart and her lashes too stubby, not like Kathy's. Elly thought about the pure sapphire blue of Kathy's eyes and the thick, luxurious lashes that had framed them. Absently, she raised the eye shadow pencil and drew a moustache on her reflection. Next she drew exaggerated lashes and brows over her mirrored eyes.

"Better," she said aloud. Her eyes moved to the remainder of the mirror and the surrounding spotless tile. Fresh paint had covered over the usual graffiti. It annoyed Elly. She took the eye shadow pencil and drew funny faces across the surface of the entire mirror.

"Needs color," she mused and fumbled in her purse for her lip gloss. She opened it up and, with her finger, drew bright pink flowers around the faces.

Elly stared at her creation, then smeared the pink and green together with her hand. She wiped it on the clean wall. Then she took the pencil again and doodled along the wall and on the fronts of the toilet stall doors. She took her lip gloss and drew flowers on the paper towel holder and on the soap dispensers. In minutes, the room was draped in pink and green. Elly let out a strange giggle and looked at her handiwork with a smirk. "Perfect," she said.

"Not so perfect," a voice said behind her. Elly spun around. A heavy feeling was growing in her stomach. Mrs. Wenzel stood at the doorway, her arms crossed and her toe tapping. "What's the meaning of this, Elly?"

The eye shadow and the lip gloss slipped from her hand and clattered to the floor. The rattling sound echoed inside her head. Her voice wouldn't work.

"I think you'd better come with me, Elly. We'll have to tell the principal what you've done. And then we'll call your parents to come and get you. You know, you could be suspended for this."

Filled with dread, Elly gathered her belongings and mutely followed Mrs. Wenzel down the hallway to the principal's office.

* * * * *

"I don't believe it." Mr. Rowan's comment was low and grim. "Is this true, Elly? Did you do this?"

Elly hung her head and stared at the brown carpet in Mr. Grant's office. They'd called her dad off a construction site when they couldn't reach her mother. His work shirt was soaked with sweat and covered with a fine white dust.

"Look at me when I'm talking to you, young lady."

The growl in her dad's tone caused Elly's head to snap up. She glared at him defiantly. "I was only having a little fun. . . ."

"Fun? Since when is it fun to destroy school property?"

Mr. Grant cleared his throat. "Mr. Rowan, I understand what Elly's been going through these past few months, what with the death of her sister and all."

Mike's expression turned stony. "There's no excuse for what she did."

"I agree," Mr. Grant said. "Elly's been a model student for years and even though I could suspend her, I'm going to be lenient because of all she's been through."

"She should be punished."

Elly heard the anger in her father's voice.

"Oh, she'll have to clean it up. And she'll get no privileges for the rest of the school year, but I won't suspend her this time."

Elly felt tears behind her eyes, but she refused to let them go. She almost wished the principal had suspended her. When the story got around about what she'd done, everyone would be talking about her and pointing at her.

"You bet she'll clean it up," Mr. Rowan said. "I'll supervise the job myself." He stood to leave and Elly struggled up beside him.

Mr. Grant stopped them before they reached the door. "Mr. Rowan, I know life's been very difficult for your family since . . . since the loss of your daughter. It was a terrible tragedy. Mrs. Wenzel suggested that perhaps some family counseling might be helpful. . . ."

"My family is just fine, Mr. Grant." Elly saw her father's knuckles go white on the door knob.

"Perfectly fine students don't go about destroying school property, Mr. Rowan."

"It won't happen again, Mr. Grant." Mr. Rowan gave Elly a threatening glare. "I know you're trying to help, but what Elly did was a stupid prank. Nothing more. Now, I'll take my daughter home. We'll be back after school and she'll clean the bathroom."

They left the school, Elly trailing behind the tense, muscular frame of her father. She felt numb all over, numb and all alone.

* * * * *

Elly sat by herself in the cafeteria, munching a tasteless sandwich. She surveyed the room and heard the kids laughter, their chatter, and the clank of their silverware against trays. *What's happening to me?* she thought to herself. She couldn't concentrate in class. She didn't want anyone trying to be her friend. They felt sorry for her. The whole world felt sorry for "poor Elly." She felt far away from everything.

Her father's disgust about her prank had followed her into her school routine. No matter how hard she tried, she couldn't forget how badly she'd disappointed her father. The kids whispering behind her back didn't help either. She felt friendless.

Elly saw Dan Richards with a plastic tray heaped with food and extra cartons of milk coming toward her. He was headed for a table full of his buddies. She noticed Kenny was sitting with them. Suddenly, Dan Richards's presence annoyed her tremendously. He had snubbed Joy. Joy had liked him, and he'd ignored her. Who was he to snub Elly's best friend anyway?

Feeling nasty, Elly slid her crutch sideways, directly in the path of Dan Richards. He didn't see it, because he was calling to his friends. His foot hooked around it perfectly. His tray flipped over in the air, and he fell sprawling to the floor. The plates, the milk, and the silverware landed in a gooey heap, and Dan slid several feet as his palms slushed through mashed potatoes. The noise stopped all the activity in the room. Every head turned.

Elly pretended to be horrified and apologized over and over. She grabbed for napkins and thrust them at Dan as he struggled off the floor. "It's okay," Dan kept saying, wiping food off his jeans. "I didn't see your crutch. It was my fault."

Elly tried to calm the racing of her pulse and pretend as if she was innocent. "It was an accident," she said. "I'm so sorry. . . ." After the janitor arrived to mop up the mess and Dan left, Elly stood and smiled inwardly over her success. Dan had believed her. The thought that he'd been so easy to fool was amusing. She gripped her crutches beneath her arms and turned around. She found herself staring straight into the knowing expression of Mrs. Wenzel.

* * * * *

"Is it true, Elly? Did you trip Dan on purpose?" Mrs. Rowan searched Elly's eyes for the truth.

Elly paced back and forth in front of her parents in the living room. Mr. Rowan straddled the edge of the sofa cushion, looking too tense to speak. Elly glanced miserably down at her plaster cast. "It was an accident," she lied.

"That's not what your teacher said. She said you did it deliberately. Why, Elly? Why would you do such a thing?"

"You never believe me! It's my word against hers."

"I believe *her*." Mr. Rowan snapped. "I saw what you did to the restroom, remember? I believe you tripped that boy just to be mean."

Hot tears sprang to Elly's eyes. "So what if I did? I know I'm rotten. I know I'm not perfect like Kathy." Her voice grew shrill. Words rushed out of her mouth she couldn't stop or control. "Don't you see? *I* should have died in the car wreck. Kathy was the smart one, the perfect one, the one you loved best. I should have died." She began to choke and gag over the tears catching in her throat. "Why wasn't it me, Daddy? Why did she have to die? Why wasn't it me instead of Kathy?"

Twelve

THE words kept tumbling out of Elly's mouth. She kept seeing Kathy's hair flying over the front seat of the car. She heard again the crunch of metal, the shattering of glass.

Helen sprang from the sofa and caught Elly in her arms. "Oh, honey. Oh, my dear Elly. Don't say such things. We love you, Elly. We love you."

Her father's face went pale, and Elly buried her face in her mother's shoulder to avoid the pain in his expression.

"I miss her so much, Mom. I want Kathy to come home."

"I know, Elly." Her mother stroked Elly's hair, smoothing the short wisps off her forehead. "We miss her, too. But Elly, you're as dear and precious to us as Kathy was. Don't ever forget that."

Elly pulled away, sniffed, and took the

handkerchief her father offered her. Late afternoon sun streamed through the windows of the living room, casting long shadows on the pale blue carpet. The shadows danced and flickered with the movement of the wind. "It—it isn't fair. Why did Kathy die instead of me? Why?"

"Elly." Mrs. Rowan pulled on Elly's hand, forcing her to look into her misted eyes. "No one can answer that question. No human mind can ever understand why bad things happen to people, why people die before their time." Mrs. Rowan's voice broke, but she cleared her throat and continued.

"All we do know is that life is for the living. You *are* here. And we are so grateful that you are." Mrs. Rowan straightened her shoulders. "Elly, we've put off something for a long time, something we should have started when you were still in the hospital. There are doctors and groups of people who help families like us, families who've lost a child."

Mr. Rowan opened his mouth to speak, but Mrs. Rowan shot him a warning glance. "We should have gotten help from people like that from the very first, but sometimes you can fool yourself. You tell yourself 'Hey, I'm all right. I can handle this.' We didn't believe we needed to talk it out. I see now that it was a mistake.

You need to talk to a counselor. We need to talk with other parents who've gone through this. We've put it off far too long, and you've suffered for it. We must start with a support group as soon as possible. All of us. Will you go, Elly? Please?"

Elly felt tired and drained. "Whatever you say, Mom. I'll do anything you say."

* * * * *

"Do you know what a support group is, Elly?" The question came from Dr. Anita Nash. Elly shook her head, her mouth too dry to speak.

"It's a group of people—in your case, other kids—who've also lost a loved one."

Elly felt herself resisting the idea. She didn't want to talk to a bunch of strange kids about her private feelings. She refused to meet Dr. Nash's eyes. Instead, she stared across the sunny office at the diplomas hanging on the wall. The walls were coral, and there were clay pots of thick green ferns beside the golden oak furniture. The room felt cozy. Elly decided that the office suited the tall, slim psychiatrist with the dark curls and open, friendly smile.

"Am I crazy, Dr. Nash?" Elly blurted out

the question suddenly. She clapped her hand over her mouth to keep other fears from spilling out.

Anita Nash smiled, her warm brown eyes softening. "Elly, a person can't go through what you went through and not have problems. Nothing is more traumatic than losing a member of one's family."

"But Kathy died weeks ago."

"How long has your leg been in a cast?"

"Since—since the accident."

"Your emotions were hurt just like your leg was, Elly. Would you expect them to heal any quicker?"

Elly pondered the doctor's words. They made sense. The pain in her heart hurt far more than her leg ever had. "How long before I forget?"

Anita Nash reached out and touched the back of Elly's hand, which was clutched tightly in her lap. "You may never forget. But you will be able to come to grips with your grief and live on in spite of it. Accepting death comes in stages."

"I don't know what you mean."

"Let me explain. First, there's denial." Elly recalled not believing her parents when they'd told her about Kathy in the hospital. "Next comes anger, then grief, and finally, acceptance. There's no time limit on how long any one stage will last. Frankly, you're still feeling anger. That's why you've been acting the way you have. You're a very angry girl, Elly Rowan."

"I still don't want to sit around and talk about it with a bunch of strangers."

"Just one visit, Elly. That's all I'm asking. Come one time and meet the others. Your parents will be attending an adult support group and each of you will be stronger for it. Sometimes, people need help from other people. Give it a chance. You won't be sorry."

* * * * *

A group of ten kids sat around a conference table in Dr. Nash's other office. They looked up curiously when Dr. Nash introduced Elly, but everyone smiled and greeted her as if they already knew her. Elly took a chair shyly, determined to make herself as unnoticeable as possible. "How was your week, Jamie?" Dr. Nash directed her question to a plump boy of about eleven.

Jamie pushed his glasses up the bridge of his nose and grinned. "Okay. I wrote down my feelings, like you said, about what I thought about when my brother died."

"Tell us about it."

Jamie thumbed through some papers in front of him. "Sam was four when he got cancer. I felt real sorry for him. And scared because I didn't want it to happen to me. I was glad it wasn't me, but sorry because I was glad."

An electric current shot up Elly's spine. That's how she'd felt, too. Secretly, she'd been glad she hadn't died, yet sorry that she felt glad.

Jamie continued. "All the time Sam was in the hospital, everybody gave him presents and lots of attention. They forgot about me. Nobody cared—not even my parents." Jamie blinked and let his next words out in a rush. "Sometimes I wanted him to hurry up and die so I could have Mom and Dad back again."

Elly glanced around the table and saw kids nodding their heads in understanding. Jamie's honesty shocked her. Was it possible to feel that way? She thought about all the times she wished she were as pretty and popular as Kathy. She remembered how she sometimes felt jealous when her father had given Kathy special attention.

"Then when Sam did die, I couldn't stop crying." Jamie's voice sounded small. "I thought I had wished him dead."

"But that's not possible, is it, Jamie?" Dr. Nash asked.

A sheepish smile crossed Jamie's face. "No. Sam died of cancer."

By the time the hour was up, Elly had heard several of the kids share their feelings and she felt strangely at ease. When the group had shared jokes, Elly had laughed, really laughed, for the first time in weeks. She felt very close to them, even though she had just met them. They were all different, but they were all alike, too. They'd all lost someone special to them. When Dr. Nash asked her if she would come to the next meeting, Elly agreed. She would be back. The group was already a part of her. It felt as she did, hurt as she did. Elly realized that she wasn't alone anymore.

* * * * *

"We'll have this thing off in two shakes, Elly," Dr. Jones announced. A tiny saw cut through the hard plaster surface of Elly's cast. Her stomach knotted. She hoped he didn't slip and cut her leg.

Mr. Rowan watched intently as the saw did its work. Elly sat perched on the stainless steel table, her leg propped straight as Dr. Jones bent over his task.

"There! It's sliced through," Dr. Jones said. He gripped the broken cast on either side of the cuts with a special tool that spread the hard plaster into two halves. "Here you go, Elly. A brand new leg."

"Ugh!" Elly wrinkled her nose. "It stinks."

"It'll wash up."

Her leg felt so light that she thought it would float off the table. "How come it looks so scrawny?" Fear seized her as she stared at her spindly-looking appendage.

"Your muscles have shriveled because you haven't used them. You'll build them up again and in a few months, it'll look just like the other one. The top layer of skin will peel and come off, so be careful if you go sunbathing. You can get a real burn on it. And don't scrub it too hard. That's fresh, new skin. You can damage it if you're not careful."

"What's she supposed to do for exercise?" Mr. Rowan asked.

"Walk a lot," Dr. Jones said. "No roller skating or downhill skiing for a while," he chuckled. "By the end of the summer, you'll never know it had been broken."

Elly looked over her leg carefully. She saw tiny scars on either side of her knee where Dr. Jones had operated. The scars would always be there. They would always remind her of the accident and the day Kathy died.

* * * * *

"Hey, Elly. You look normal again." A wide grin split Kenny's face as he approached Elly in the hall. Her heart fluttered. Ever since the dance, she'd felt awkward around Kenny. She'd wanted to apologize but wasn't sure how.

"Thanks." She thought he looked especially handsome in the chocolate brown polo shirt.

"How're things going?" he asked.

Her first instinct was to fake a smile and say, "Just fine," as she always did. But the support group had taught her that it was all right to tell her true feelings. Instead, she said, "Some days are better than others."

Kenny nodded. "So what are you going to do this summer?"

School would be out at the end of the week. The thought of summer frightened Elly. What would she do? How would it be to not have Kathy? "Hang around," she answered.

"Me too," Kenny confessed. "Dad's talking about a vacation to Disney World." He rolled his eyes. "Can you imagine two weeks in a car with my bratty brothers and my dad grumbling all the way?"

A lump rose in Elly's throat. "I wish I could."

Kenny's face reddened. He slid his hands into the back pockets of his jeans. "I—I'm sorry, Elly. I didn't think." He looked like he wanted to bolt.

Elly smiled, "It's all right. Every day is better than the last one." It was the truth. Her anger was leaving her, replaced by sadness. Nothing could bring Kathy back. Elly left Kenny standing alone in the hall and walked swiftly into her classroom.

Thirteen

"MOM, I want you to take me to Kathy's grave. I've never been there. Dr. Nash says that because I was in the hospital during her funeral, I never got to say good-bye." Elly's request had stopped her mother in mid-step in the kitchen. School was out for the summer. Although it was only nine in the morning, the temperature was climbing outside. The kitchen fan hummed noisily.

"Are you sure you want to go?"

"I'm sure."

They drove to the cemetery before noon, entering through the wrought-iron gates and winding down the road, past the bright green grass. Elly clutched a clump of wildflowers against her lap. Hues of lavender, yellow, and blue glimmered in the sunlight as it poured through the car window.

She thought the grounds were beautiful

and peaceful, shaded by weeping willows. Vases of flowers stood like exclamation marks, in row after row. Elly's anticipation grew as their car curved past fields of plaques and simple headstones. She wanted to see Kathy's, but at the same time, she didn't. One of the girls in her support group had told her, "I think I accepted my mother's death when I saw her gravestone. Up until then, I kept thinking it wasn't real."

The car halted and Mrs. Rowan pointed across a wide expanse of lawn toward an ash tree. "It's over there, to the right of the tree. Do you want me to come with you?"

Elly decided to go alone and crossed the green lawn. She glanced to the right and left at names she didn't know. The warm summer sun beat on her bare shoulders. She'd worn a pale yellow sundress because Kathy would have been pleased to see her without her usual funky garb.

Elly saw a bronze plaque, ringed by an etching of bronze flowers. Her heart thudded. *Kathleen Anne Rowan*, it read, along with the date of birth and death. That was all. It was so simple that tears formed in Elly's eyes.

Her hands shook. She stooped and traced the raised letters with her fingers. She lay the wilting bouquet very carefully at the bottom of the marker, just under Kathy's name.

Elly breathed in the smell of freshly mown grass. A brilliant blue sky sparkled down, decorated by puffy white clouds. The sound of sprinklers broke the quiet.

"Good-bye, Kathy. I love you." Elly rose slowly, wiping the back of her hand across her cheek. "I wish I could talk to you." She backed off, knowing that her mother waited in the hot car. She should go. She'd said her farewells. She started toward the car, then turned once more to see her sister's grave.

In the distance, a sprinkler spun. As the rays of the sun shot through the water, something wonderful happened. A rainbow formed, perfectly positioned in the air over Kathy's grave. The sight made Elly catch her breath. She watched as the shimmering droplets caught the sun and spilled their beauty onto the grass below.

* * * * *

The strains of "Happy Birthday" faded. Elly leaned forward and puffed heavily on the fourteen candles on her birthday cake. The flames died, and her mother flipped on the kitchen light. Mr. Rowan and Joy applauded happily.

"Not bad, Elly. You got them all in one puff," her father said. "I always said you were full of hot air."

"Daddy!" Elly wailed, but beamed at his teasing smile.

"Let me cut it," Mrs. Rowan said, sliding a knife through the thick chocolate frosting.

Elly remembered other birthdays. Kathy had always teased, "You'll never catch up with me, little sister." And Elly had always answered, "Well, you'll be thirty before me." Only months before, Kathy's birthday had come and gone. They'd tiptoed around mentioning it, but the atmosphere had weighed heavy in the house. Now it was Elly's special day and she'd invited Joy to share it with her.

"I want to open my presents."

"Presents?" Mr. Rowan teased. "What makes you think you're getting cake AND presents?"

"Open mine first," Joy urged, thrusting a brightly wrapped box at Elly.

She tore the paper off and squealed with delight. "A new cassette. Thanks, Joy." Her parents had given her a gift certificate for new clothes that morning. She wasn't expecting anything else. But her dad pulled out a second box from beneath the table.

"Gee, for me?" She couldn't conceal her surprise.

Mr. Rowan shrugged. "Just something I picked out in one of those fancy stores. The saleslady said it was the height of fashion."

She imagined him entering a women's department of a store, his big, broad shoulders amid all the dainty female things. The image touched her heart. Elly tore open the flat box and discovered several pairs of socks. She blinked at the bright colors.

A lump rose in Elly's throat. She smoothed her hand over the socks and gave her father a loving look. His brown eyes twinkled at her. A silly grin tipped the corners of his mouth. She saw the dimples hiding in his cheeks. Kathy had inherited his dimples. "I really like them, Daddy. Thank you very much."

He tugged on a hank of her hair playfully. She felt closer to him than she had in months. "You're welcome, baby girl."

When he picked up his fork to eat his cake, Elly saw a glimpse of herself in his profile. At that moment she loved him more than she ever had before. She realized that in his way he'd said he loved her, too. She wanted to throw her arms around him and tell him, but instead she laughed aloud, a deep laugh that bubbled up from inside her heart.

* * * * *

"I don't think it's fair that girls get to cry and boys aren't supposed to." The angry observation came from Al, nineteen, the oldest member of Elly's support group. "Why is it sissy for boys to cry? It hurts us just as badly when someone we love dies."

Elly looked at Al's pained expression. Guiltily, she remembered the night she'd heard her father crying. She'd thought the same thing.

"I'm sorry that our society is that way," Dr. Nash said. "You're absolutely right, Al. Crying is a natural reaction to pain. Boys shouldn't be made to feel that tears are wrong or foolish or sissy."

"When my father died," Al continued, "I became the man of the house. I had to drop out of college and move back home. It's been tough, but my mom and my brother and sisters needed me."

Elly measured Al with awe. He was only five years older than she, yet he was responsible for his whole family. She glanced from person to person. She felt a warmth from them, almost like they were family.

"When my best friend died, I didn't cry at all," Betty, a twelve year old said. "But when my cat died, I couldn't stop crying. I cried for days. That's when my parents made me come here."

"Grief is an odd thing," Dr. Nash confirmed. "Sometimes we act very strangely. Good students get into trouble at school." Elly identified with her comment. "Or we do bizarre things."

"Like smearing makeup all over the girls' bathroom," Elly announced.

The kids at the table laughed. "Or spreading peanut butter all over my mom's kitchen walls," another girl said.

"Or throwing all my brother's toys out the upstairs window after he died," Jamie added.

"The ability to mourn—grieve—and then go on with your lives is the most important emotional experience you can have." Dr. Nash told them. "People who don't mourn may never fully recover from their loss."

Elly pondered Dr. Nash's words. She would miss Kathy forever. The sadness, the sense of loss, the feelings of being unloved and isolated had wounded her. But she felt better after every support group meeting. The road to feeling normal again was long, but she was glad she was on it, surrounded by people who really understood and cared.

Fourteen

ELLY picked up the newspaper and read:

FOR SALE: Complete French Provincial bedroom suite. Canopy bed, dresser with mirror, bureau and night stand. Like new condition.

A strange feeling crept through her. Her parents were selling Kathy's bedroom furniture. They'd discussed it for a week. "I can make it into a sewing room," her mother had said. Elly agreed with the decision. Yet, seeing the actual words printed on paper made her feel strangely.

As she entered her sister's room, she somehow still expected to find Kathy there. Kathy's clothes had been donated to charity. Her personal things had been packed away for later years. Elly had kept Kathy's photos, her records, her diary, and many of her books. All that remained was the furniture. And after that was gone, all traces of Kathy's physical presence would be gone.

She'd told the support group about it. Many kids had nodded knowingly, telling her what it had been like for them to see the things that belonged to their loved ones disappear. "At first I felt like Dad was trying to pretend that Mom had never existed. You know—erase her from our lives. But later it was easier than looking at her stuff day after day," an older girl had told the group.

Every time the phone rang, Elly jumped. But her mother took all the calls. Early that evening, a couple pulled up towing a trailer. They came inside and looked at the bedroom set with shining eyes. "We'll take it," they said.

"Our daughter, Melissa, has wanted a canopy bed ever since she was four. She'll be ten tomorrow." Mrs. Baer said.

"These pieces are in great condition," Mr. Baer commented. "They hardly seem used."

Kathy had gotten it for her twelfth birthday. It had been her proudest possession. Elly leaned against the door frame and watched the Baers circle the room. She fought against resenting them.

"Are you tired of the furniture, dear?" Mrs. Baer asked.

Elly darted her eyes from her mother to her father. "Uh—this isn't my room. It was my sister's." She watched Mr. Baer as he wrote a check and handed it to her dad.

"Oh, you have another daughter? Has she moved away?"

"Yes," Helen smiled kindly. "She's moved away."

Elly was relieved that her mother hadn't blurted out the truth. For some reason, she didn't want these strangers to know their private business.

"You must miss her," Mrs. Baer commented.

"Very much. But we're adjusting."

"Here, I'll give you a hand," Mr. Rowan said, stooping to pick up the night stand. He lifted it effortlessly and went down the stairs. The lifting and hauling continued until every piece of furniture was in the trailer.

At the curb, Mr. Baer held out his hand. "Thanks for your help, Mr. Rowan. I know how much Melissa will appreciate this."

Mr. Rowan shook his hand, and Elly stepped next to him. His arm slid around her shoulders and held her tightly against his side.

The Baers climbed into their car and started the engine. "Tell your daughter how much having her furniture means to us when you see her. We'll take very good care of it."

"I'll tell her." Mr. Rowan waved as the car pulled away. Elly stood close to him, looking down the stretch of road long after the car had vanished. Dusk was settling over the neighborhood, and fireflies blinked in the gathering night.

*　*　*　*　*

The morning sunlight splashed across the pink carpet of the empty room. Elly slipped inside and settled against the wall nearest the door. Her gaze looked to the corners of Kathy's former bedroom. She hadn't planned on coming to the room until after her mom had fixed it up. But she'd come anyway, in spite of herself.

The carpet needed vacuuming. Little balls of dust lay where the bed had stood. Lint fluttered in the rays of the flooding sunshine. Elly saw the stain in the far corner where she'd accidently spilled Kathy's fingernail polish.

"Oh, no! I ruined your rug!" Elly's eyes brimmed with tears. *"Mom will kill me."*

Kathy sopped up the mess with a tissue. "Stop crying about it and help me clean it up.

Get the polish remover."

Elly obeyed, but when she sponged it into the carpet, the pretty pink color came out, too. "What else can go wrong?"

"It's all right, Elly." Kathy patted her hand. "I never liked that shade of pink anyway."

Elly saw the place where the mirror had hung. The faint outline etched into the wallpaper had been faded by strong sunlight through the years.

Kathy studied her face intently in the mirror. Elly pondered what could be so fascinating about sizing up one's reflection hour after hour. "Don't you ever stop staring at yourself in the mirror?" she asked.

"Someday when you're thirteen and not a kid anymore, you'll stare at yourself, too."

Miffed, Elly asked, "What's the big deal? You better wipe off that eye shadow before Daddy sees it."

"I like it." Kathy tipped her chin to stare at the bright slash of blue across her eyelids. "David Johnson kissed me at Beth's party last night."

Elly's mouth dropped open. "He did?"

"We were playing a kissing game."

"Daddy would ground you forever if he knew."

"But no one's going to tell him, is she?"

Kathy's look was threatening.

Elly puckered. "Did he kiss like a fish?"

"Like a puppy with a wet tongue."

Elly laughed, flopping onto Kathy's bed and turning a somersault. "I'm going to tell him what you said."

"Grow up, Elly. Someday you'll kiss a boy and tell me all about it. And I won't tease you."

Elly circled the room slowly, the walls whispering to her. She thought the memories would make her sad. Instead, they made her feel closer to Kathy.

"Elly. Don't be silly. There's no such thing as a Tooth Fairy." Seven-year-old Kathy put her hands on her hips and gave her sister an exasperated sigh.

"There is too! Look at this." Elly opened her fat fingers and showed her a shiny quarter. *"And see."* She opened her mouth to show Kathy the hole in front where her tooth had fallen out.

"You're only six, Elly Rowan. Don't you think I know more about these things than you?"

Elly completed the tour of the empty room. She paused at the door for one long, last, lingering glance. Finally she stepped quietly into the hall and snapped the door closed behind her.

Fifteen

"**WHY** is July so hot?" Elly muttered under her breath as she walked down the sidewalks of her neighborhood. The exercise was paying off. Her leg was stronger everyday.

Overhead, leaves drooped, limp from heat and too little rain. Shadows darted just in front of her on the sidewalk. She wondered why a person never caught up with her shadow. She took a giant step to prove her theory. Her shadow moved forward, always just ahead of her.

"Hey, Elly! Wait up." At the sound of her name, Elly turned. Kenny Hughes jogged from the corner and fell into step beside her. As usual, he looked terrific. She felt the familiar pangs and flutter of her pulse over his closeness.

"I thought it was you," Kenny said, with a

winded smile. Her heart did a funny flip-flop.

"Welcome home. How was Disney World?" Her flowered shirt stuck to her back. She lifted her hair off her collar and fanned her neck. Maybe her hair would be long again by the time school started.

"Pretty neat. I spent all my time on Space Mountain. It's pitch dark, and you go zooming up and down on a giant roller coaster."

She shivered, not sure if it was over his description or over his nearness. "You got a tan."

"When I wasn't on Space Mountain, I was at the pool." He bent and plucked a blade of grass and chewed it. "I see your leg's better."

"I have to walk every day to build up the muscles." Her turquoise shorts hugged her thighs, and she gave the hem a self-conscious tug. "I almost don't notice the scars at my knee anymore."

Their path had brought them to the front of the school building. "Want to rest?" he asked, leading her over to a large shade tree. She settled her back against the bark of the tree. He sat in front of her, his legs crossed, Indian fashion. Light filtered through the tree branches and cast a sprinkling of sun and shadows on his hair.

"Ready for school to start?" Kenny asked.

"Never! How about you?"

"It's better than sitting around staring at the tube." He pulled up another blade of grass and trailed it along her nose and cheek. It tickled and she felt her face grow warm. "Are you okay now?" His voice showed concern.

She knew he wasn't asking about her leg again. "I've been going to a special support group," she said. She surprised herself that she'd told anyone other than Joy. "It's been a big help."

Kenny nodded solemnly. "I wished I could have gone to one when my grandfather died."

His words caught her off-guard. "What do you mean?"

"Oh, when I was ten, my grandfather died. He'd lived with us all my life, ever since I'd been a baby. He was my best friend." Kenny's eyes grew distant, as if viewing something inside his head. "He always took me fishing. For my tenth birthday, he was supposed to take me out to the ocean. We planned it for weeks. Then one morning he didn't wake up."

Elly nibbled on her lower lip. She saw the same hurt in his eyes as she saw in the eyes of every person in her support group. "I'll bet you were angry at him for not taking you fishing."

Kenny blinked, wide-eyed at her. "Yeah.

How'd you know? I mean, wasn't that a terrible thing to think about? That I wasn't going to go fishing when my grandfather—my very best buddy—had just died?"

"What did you do?" Elly asked.

"My folks wouldn't let me go to the funeral. They thought it would bother me too much."

"It might have helped," Elly said.

"Probably. Because I didn't see him again, I didn't really believe that he wouldn't come take me fishing. He'd never broken a promise. So on my birthday, I got up very early and got dressed. I sat on the back porch with my fishing gear and waited." A frown puckered Kenny's forehead. "Of course, he didn't come."

A lump rose in Elly's throat, imagining Kenny as a boy, waiting for a man who would never arrive. "Of course, I wouldn't be that way if it happened now," Kenny said. "But whenever I smell pipe tobacco I think of him. And, you know, I still miss him."

Elly knew. She waited while Kenny gathered his feelings. When he looked at her again, his ears were slightly red. "I never told anybody that story before."

"I'll never forget Kathy," she said, attempting to make him feel more comfortable for sharing his secret. "I know that she was smarter and prettier than I am. I used to think that Mom and Dad loved her more than me, too. But I'd give anything in the world if she could come back home again."

The day had turned quiet and soft. Above them, shadow patterns twirled and danced as a breeze riffled the leaves. The scent of honeysuckle filled the air. Kenny's fingers touched the side of Elly's face. "She was very pretty," he confirmed. "But so are you."

Elly's mouth went dry as she stared into his bright blue eyes. He leaned forward, hesitated, then leaned closer and kissed her gently on the mouth. Sun chased the shadows from the corners of her mind, and Elly Rowan smiled.

If you would like more information about support groups for parents and children who are grieving over the loss of a child or sibling, contact:

Compassionate Friends, Inc.
P.O. Box 3696
Oak Brook, IL 60522

About the Author

LURLENE MCDANIEL made up her first story in second grade, wrote a play in fourth grade, and wrote a book in high school. She graduated from college and became a copywriter, writing ad campaigns for hundreds of clients. Now, when Lurlene is not writing books, she writes a column on writing for a Christian magazine, and teaches writing courses and seminars.

Young readers from all over the country write to Lurlene to say how much they enjoy her books. They often ask the question, "Where do you get your ideas?" Lurlene says that ideas are everywhere, on television news programs, in newspapers, and even in her own children. She uses her family and friends as character samples. Her background includes modeling, television, and a fondness for horses.

Writing books about kids overcoming sensitive problems like cancer, diabetes, and divorce draw a wide response from her readers. Yet, Lurlene says the highest compliment a reader can give her is, "Your story was so interesting that I couldn't put it down." Lurlene adds that basically, that's what writing is all about—writing an uplifting story that causes the reader to look at life from a different perspective.

Lurlene and her husband live in Tallahassee, Florida with their two sons, who are both active soccer players.

Other books by Lurlene McDaniel include *Six Months to Live, If I Should Die Before I Wake*, and *Sometimes Love Just Isn't Enough*.